T0145807

Peter Whiffle

Peter Whiffle

His Life and Works

Carl Van Vechten

MINT EDITIONS

Peter Whiffle: His Life and Works was first published in 1922.

This edition published by Mint Editions 2021.

ISBN 9781513282268 | E-ISBN 9781513287287

Published by Mint Editions®

 MINT
EDITIONS
minteditionbooks .com

Publishing Director: Jennifer Newens
Design & Production: Rachel Lopez Metzger
Project Manager: Micaela Clark
Typesetting: Westchester Publishing Services

To the memory of
My Mother,
Ada Amanda Fitch Van Vechten

"'Tingling is the test,' said Babbalanja, 'Yoomy, did you tingle, when that song was composing?'"
"'All over, Babbalanja.'"

Herman Melville: Mardi

"We work in the dark—we do what we can—we give what we have. Our doubt is our passion, and our passion is our task. The rest is the madness of art."

Dencombe: The Middle Years

"Les existences les plus belles sont peut-être celles qui ont subi tous les extrêmes, qui ont traversé toutes les températures, rencontré toutes les sensations excessives et tous les sentiments contradictoires."

Remy de Gourmont: Le Chat de Misère

"The man who satisfies a ceaseless intellectual curiosity probably squeezes more out of life in the long run than any one else."

Edmund Gosse: Books on the Table

"O mother of the hills, forgive our towers;
O mother of the clouds, forgive our dreams."

Edwin Ellis

CONTENTS

PREFACE

So few people were acquainted with Peter Whiffle that the announcement, on that page of the New York Times consecrated to wedding, birth, and obituary notices, of his death in New York on December 15, 1919, awakened no comment. Those of my friends who knew something of the relationship between Peter and myself, probably did not see the slender paragraph at all. At any rate none of them mentioned it, save, of course, Edith Dale, whose interest, in a sense, was as special as my own. Her loss was not so personal, however, nor her grief so deep. It was strange and curious to remember that however infrequently we had met, and the chronicle which follows will give evidence of the comparative infrequency of these meetings, yet some indestructible bond, a firm determining girdle of intimate understanding, over which Time and Space had no power, held us together. I had become to Peter something of a necessity, in that through me he found the proper outlet for his artistic explosions. I was present, indeed, at the bombing of more than one discarded theory. It was under the spell of such apparently trivial and external matters that our friendship developed and, while my own interests often flew in other directions, Peter certainly occupied as important a place in my heart as I did in his, probably, in some respects, more important. Nevertheless, when I received a notification from his lawyer that I had been mentioned in Peter's will, I was considerably astonished. My astonishment increased when I was informed of the nature of the bequest. Peter Whiffle had appointed me to serve as his literary executor.

Now Peter Whiffle was not, in any accepted sense of the epithet, an author. He had never published a book; he had never, indeed, written a book. In the end he had come to hold a somewhat mystic theory in regard to such matters, which he had only explained to me a few moments before he died. I was, however, aware, more aware than any one else could possibly have been, that from time to time he had been accustomed to take notes. I was as familiar, I suppose, as any one could be, with the trend of his later ideas, and with some of the major incidents in his earlier life he had acquainted me, although, here, I must confess, there were lacunæ in my knowledge. Still, his testamentary request, unless I might choose to accept it in a sense, I am convinced, entirely too flattering to my slender talents, seemed to be inconsistent with the speculative idea which haunted him, at least towards the end of his life. This contradiction and an enlarging sense of the mysterious character of the assignment were somewhat dispelled by a letter, dated June 17, 1917, which, a few days after the reading of the will, his lawyer placed in my hands and which indicated plainly enough that Peter had decided upon my appointment at least two years and a half before he died. This letter not only confirmed the strange clause in the will but also, to some extent, explained it and, as the letter is an essential part of my narrative, I offer it in evidence at once.

Dear Carl—so it read:

I suppose that some day I shall die; people do die. If there has been one set purpose in my life, it has been not to have a purpose. That, you alone, perhaps, understand. You know how I have always hesitated to express myself definitely, you know how I have refrained from writing, and you also know, perhaps, that I can write; indeed, until recently, you thought I was writing, or would write. But I think you realize now what writing has come to mean to me, definition, constant definition, although it is as apparent as anything can be that life, nature, art, whatever one writes about, are fluid and mutable things, perpetually undergoing change and, even when they assume some semblance of permanence, always presenting two or more faces. There are those who are not appalled by these conditions, those who confront them with bravery and even with impertinence. You have been courageous. You have published several books which I have read with varying shades of pleasure, and you have not hesitated to define, or at any rate discuss, even that intangible, invisible, and noisy art called Music.

I have begun many things but nothing have I ever completed. It has always seemed unnecessary or impossible, although at times I have tried to carry a piece of work through. On these occasions a restraining angel has held me firmly back. It might be better if what I have written, what I have said, were permitted to pass into oblivion with me, to become a part of scoriac chaos. It may not mean anything in particular; if it means too much, to that extent I have failed.

Thinking, however, of death, as I sometimes do, I have wondered if, after all, behind the vapoury curtain of my fluctuating purpose, behind the orphic wall of my indecision, there did not lurk some vague shadow of intention. Not on my part, perhaps, but on the part of that being, or that condition, which is reported to be interested in such matters. This doubt, I confess, I owe to you. Sometimes, in those extraordinary moments between sleeping and awakening—and once in the dentist's chair, after I had taken gas—the knots seemed to unravel, the problem seemed as naked as Istar at the seventh gate. But these moments are difficult, or impossible, to recapture. To recapture them I should have been compelled to invent a new style, a style as capricious and vibratory as the moments themselves. In this, however, as you know, I have failed, while you have succeeded. It is to your success, modest as it may appear to you, that I turn in my dilemma. To come to the point, cannot you explain, make out some kind of case for me, put me on my feet (or in a book), and thereby prove or disprove something? Shameless as I am, it would be inconceivable, absurd, for me to ask you to do this while I am yet living and I have, therefore, put my request into a formal clause in my will. After I am dead, you may search your memory, which I know to be very good, for such examples of our conversations as will best be fitted to illuminate your subject, which I must insist—you, yourself, will understand this, too, sooner or later—*is not me at all.*

When your book is published, I shall be dead and perhaps unconscious. If, however, as I strongly suspect, some current connects the life to be with the life that is, I can enjoy what you have done. At the best, you may give others a slight intimation of the meaning of inspiration or furnish guideposts, lighthouses, and bell-buoys to the poet who intends to march singing along the highroad or bravely to embark on the ships at sea; at the worst, I have furnished you with a subject for another book, and I am well aware that subjects even for bad books are difficult to light upon.

Salve atque Vale,
Peter

This letter, I may say, astonished me. I think it would astonish anybody. A profound and enveloping melancholy succeeded to this feeling of astonishment. At the time, I was engaged in putting the finishing touches to The Tiger in the House and I postponed meditation on Peter's affair until that bulky volume could be dispatched to the printer. That happy event fell on March 15, 1920, but my anthology, Lords of The Housetops, next claimed my attention, and then the new edition of Interpreters, for which I had agreed to furnish a new paper, and the writing of this new paper amused me very much, carrying my mind not only far away from cats, which had been occupying it for a twelvemonth, but also away from Peter's request. At last, Interpreters was ready for the printer, but now the proofs of The Tiger began to come in, and I may say that for the next three months my days were fully occupied in the correction of proofs, for those of Lords of The Housetops and Interpreters were in my garret when the proofs of The Tiger were not. Never have I corrected proofs with so much concentrated attention as that which I devoted to the proofs of The Tiger, and yet there were errors. In regard to some of these, I was not the collaborator. On Page 240, for instance, one may read, There are many females in the novels of Emile Zola. My intention was to have the fourth word read, felines, and so it stood in the final proof, but my ambition to surmount the initial letter of Zola's Christian name with an acute accent (an ambition I shall forswear on this present page), compelled the printer to reset the line, so that subsequently, when I opened the book at this page, I read with amazement that there are many females in the novels of Emile Zola, a statement that cannot be readily denied, to be sure, but still it is no discovery of which to boast.

It was not until September, 1920, that I had an opportunity to seriously consider Peter's request and when I did begin to consider it, I thought of it at first only as a duty to be accomplished. But when I began searching my memory for details of the conversations between us and had perused certain notes I had made on various occasions, visited his house on Beekman Place to look over his effects and talk with his mother, the feeling of the artist for *inevitable* material came over me and I knew that whether Peter had written me that letter or not, I should sooner or later have written this book about him.

There was another struggle over the eventual form, a question concerning which Peter had made no suggestions. It seemed to me, at first, that a sort of haphazard collection of his ideas and pronunciamentos, somewhat in the manner of Samuel Butler's Note-Books, would meet the case, but after a little reflection I rejected this idea. Light on the man was needed for a complete understanding of his ideas, or lack of them, for they shifted like the waves of the sea. I can never tell why, but it was while I was reading William Dean Howells's Familiar Spanish Studies one day in the New York Public Library that I suddenly decided on a sort of loose biographical form, a free fantasia in the manner of a Liszt Rhapsody. This settled, I literally swam ahead and scarcely found it necessary to examine many papers (which was fortunate as few exist) or to consult anything but my memory, which lighted up the subject from obscure angles, as a search-light illuminates the spaces of the sea, once I had learned to decipher the meaning of the problem. What it is all about, or whether it is about anything at all, you, the reader, of course, must decide for yourself. To me, the moral, if I may use a conventional word to express an unconventional idea, is plain, and if I have not succeeded in making it appear so, then I must to some extent blame you, the reader, for what is true of all books, is perhaps truest of this, that you will carry away from it only what you are able to bring to it.

I

One of my friends, a lady, visited Venice alone in her middle age. It was late at night when the train drew into the station, and it was raining, a drizzly, chilling rain. The porter pushed her, with her bag, into a damp gondola and the dismal voyage to the hotel began. There were a few lights here and there but she had the impression that she was floating down the Chicago River in a wash-tub. Once she had reached her destination, she clambered unsteadily out of the black barge, wobbled through a dark passageway, inhaling great whiffs of masticated garlic, and finally emerged in a dimly lighted lobby. At the desk, a sleepy clerk yawned as she spoke of her reservation. Tired, rather cross, and wholly disappointed, she muttered, I don't like Venice at all. I wish I hadn't come. The clerk was unsympathetically explanatory, Signora should have visited Venice when she was younger.

A day or so later, the lady recovered her spirit and even her sense of humour for she told me the story herself and I have always remembered it. The moment it passed her lips, indeed, I began to reflect that I had been lucky to encounter the Bride of the Adriatic in my youth. Paris, too, especially Paris, for there is a melancholy pleasure to be derived from Venice. It is a suitable environment for grief; there is a certain superior relish to suffering there. Paris, I sometimes think, smiles only on the very young and it is not a city I should care to approach for the first time after I had passed forty.

I was, as a matter of fact, in my twenties when I first went to Paris—my happiness might have been even greater had I been nineteen—and I was alone. The trip across England—I had landed at Liverpool—and the horrid channel, I will not describe, although both made sufficient impression on me, but the French houses at Dieppe awakened my first deep emotion and then, and so many times since, the Normandy cider, quaffed in a little café, conterminous to the railroad, and the journey through France, alive in the sunlight, for it was May, the fields dancing with the green grain spattered with vermilion poppies and cerulean cornflowers, the white roads, flying like ribbons between the stately poplars, leading away over the charming hills past the red-brick villas, completed the siege of my not too easily given heart. There was the stately and romantic interruption of Rouen, which at that period suggested nothing in the world to me but Emma Bovary. Then more fields, more roads, more towns, and at last, towards twilight, Paris.

Railroads have a fancy for entering cities stealthily through backyards and the first glimpses of Paris, achieved from a car window, were not over pleasant but the posters on the hoardings, advertising beer and automobile tires, particularly that of the Michelin Tire Company, with the picture of the pinguid gentleman, constructed of a series of pneumatic circles, seemed characteristic enough. Chéret was dead but something of his spirit seemed to glow in these intensely coloured affiches and I was young. Even the dank Gare Saint Lazare did not dismay me, and I entered into the novel baggage hunt with something of zest, while other busy passengers and the blue porters rushed hither and thither in a complicated but well-ordered maze. Naturally, however, I was the last to leave the station; as the light outside deepened to a rich warm blue, I wandered into the street, my porter bearing my trunk, to find there a solitary cocher mounted on the box of his carious fiacre.

An artist friend, Albert Worcester, had already determined my destination and so I gave commands, Hotel de la Place de l'Odéon, the cocher cracked his whip, probably adding a Hue cocotte! and we were under way. The drive through the streets that evening seemed like a dream and, even later, when the streets of Paris had become more familiar to me than those of any other city, I could occasionally recapture the mood of this first vision. For Paris in the May twilight is very soft and exquisite, the grey buildings swathed in a bland blue light and the air redolent with a strange fragrance, the ingredients of which have never been satisfactorily identified in my nasal imagination, although Huysmans, Zola, Symons, and Cunninghame Graham have all attempted to separate and describe them. Presently we crossed the boulevards and I saw for the first time the rows of blooming chestnut trees, the kiosques where newsdealers dispensed their wares, the brilliantly lighted theatres, the sidewalk cafés, sprinkled with human figures, typical enough, doubtless, but who all seemed as unreal to me at the time as if they had been Brobdingnags, Centaurs, Griffins, or Mermaids. Other fiacres, private carriages, taxi-autos, carrying French men and French ladies, passed us. I saw Bel Ami, Nana, Liane de Pougy, or Otero in every one of them. As we drove by the Opéra, I am certain that Cléo de Mérode and Leopold of Belgium descended the steps. Even the buses assumed the appearance of gorgeous chariots, bearing perfumed Watteauesque ladies on their journey to Cythera.

As we drove through the Tuileries Gardens, the mood snapped for an instant as I viewed the statue of Gambetta, which, I thought at the time, and have always thought since, was amazingly like the portrait of a gentleman hailing a cab. What could more completely symbolize Paris than the statue of a gentleman perpetually hailing a cab and never getting one?

We drove on through the Louvre and now the Seine was under us, lying black in the twilight, reviving dark memories of crime and murder, on across the Pont du Carrousel, and up the narrow Rue de Seine. The Quartier Latin! I must have cried aloud, for the cocher looked a trifle suspicious, his head turned the fraction of an inch. Later, of course, I said, the left bank, as casually as any one. It was almost dark when we drove into the open Place, flanked by the Odéon, a great Roman temple, with my little hotel tucked into one corner, as unostentatiously as possible, being exactly similar to every other structure, save the central one, in the Place. I shall stop tonight, I said to myself, in the hotel where Little Billee lived, for, when one first goes to Paris when one is young, Paris is either the Paris of Murger, du Maurier, or the George Moore of the Confessions, perhaps the Paris of all three. In my bag these three books lay, and I had already begun to live one of them.

The patron and a servant in a long white apron were waiting, standing in the doorway. The servant hoisted my trunk to his shoulder and bore it away. I paid the cocher's reckoning, not without difficulty for, although I was not ignorant of the language, I was unaccustomed to the simplicity of French coinage. There were also the mysteries of the pourboire to compute—ten per cent, I had been told; who has not been told this?—and besides, as always happens when one is travelling, I had no little money. But at length the negotiations were terminated, not to the displeasure of the cocher, I feel certain, since he condescended to smile pleasantly. Then, with a crack of his whip, this enormous fellow with his black moustaches, his glazed top-hat, and his long coat, drove away. I cast a long lingering look after him, apparently quite unaware that many another such teratological specimen existed on every hand. Now I followed the patron into a dark hallway and new strata of delight. He gave me a lighted candle and, behind him, I mounted the winding stairway to the first floor, where I was deposited in a chamber with dark red walls, heavy dark red curtains at the windows, which looked out over the Place, a black walnut wash-hand-stand with pitcher and basin, a huge black walnut wardrobe, two or three chairs of the same wood, upholstered with faded brocade, and a most luxurious bed, so high from the floor that one had to climb into it, hung with curtains like those at the window, and surmounted by a featherbed. There was also another article of furniture, indispensable to any French bedroom.

I gave Joseph (all men servants in small hotels in Paris are named Joseph, perhaps to warn off prospective Potiphar's wives) his vail, asked for hot water, which he bore up promptly in a small can, washed myself, did a little unpacking, humming the Mattchiche the while, changed my shirt, my collar and my necktie, demanded another bougie, lighted it, and under the humble illumination afforded by it and its companion, I began to read again The Confessions of a Young Man. It was not very long before I was interrupted in the midst of an absorbing passage descriptive of the circle at the Nouvelle Athènes by the arrival of Albert Worcester, who had arranged for my reception, and right here I may say that I was lodged in the Hotel de la Place de l'Odéon for fifty francs a month. Albert's arrival, although unannounced, was not unexpected, as he had promised to take me to dinner.

I was sufficiently emphatic. Paris! I cried. Paris! Good God!

I see you are not disappointed. But Albert permitted a trace of cynicism to flavour his smile.

It's too perfect, too wonderful. It is more than I felt or imagined. I'm moving in.

But you haven't seen it. . .

I've seen enough. I don't mean that. I mean I've seen enough to know. But I want to see it all, everything, Saint Sulpice, the Folies-Bergère, the Musée de Cluny, the Nouvelle Athènes, the Comédie Française, the Bal Bullier, the Arc de Triomphe, the Luxembourg Gardens. . .

They close at sundown. My expression was the cue for him to continue, They'll be open tomorrow and any other day. They're just around the corner. You can go there when you get up in the morning, if you do get up in the morning. But what do you want to do tonight?

Anything! Everything! I cried.

Well, we'll eat first.

So we blew out the candles, floated down the dark stairs—I didn't really walk for a week, I am sure—, brushing on our way against a bearded student and a girl, fragrant and warm in the semi-blackness, out into the delicious night, with the fascinating indescribable odour of Paris, which ran the gamut from the fragrance of lilac and mimosa to the aroma of horse-dung; with the sound of horses' hoofs and rolling

CARL VAN VECHTEN

wheels beating and revolving on the cobble-stones, we made our way—I swear my feet never touched the ground—through the narrow, crooked, constantly turning, bewildering streets, until we came out on a broad boulevard before the Café d'Harcourt, where I was to eat my first Paris dinner.

The Café d'Harcourt is situated near the Church of the Sorbonne on the Boulevard Saint Michel, which you are more accustomed to see spelled Boul' Mich'. It is a big, brightly lighted café, with a broad terrasse, partially enclosed by a hedge of green bushes in boxes. The hands of the clock pointed to the hour of eight when we arrived and the tables all appeared to be occupied. Inside, groups of men were engaged in games of checkers, while the orchestra was performing selections from Louis Ganne's operetta, Les Saltimbanques. On the terrasse, each little table, covered with its white cloth, was lighted by a tiny lamp with a roseate shade, over which faces glowed. The bottles and dishes and silver all contributed their share to the warmth of the scene, and heaping bowls of peaches and pears and apples and little wood strawberries, ornamenting the sideboards, gave the place an almost sumptuous appearance. Later I learned that fruit was expensive in Paris and not to be tasted lightly. Victor Maurel has told me how, dining one night with the composer of The Barber, he was about to help himself to a peach from a silver platter in the centre of the table when the frugal Madame Rossini expostulated, Those are to look at, not to eat!

While we lingered on the outer sidewalk, a little comedy was enacted, through the dénouement of which we secured places. A youth, with wine in his head and love in his eyes, caressed the warm lips of an adorable girl. Save for the glasses of apéritifs from which they had been drinking, their table was bare. They had not yet dined. He clasped her tightly in his arms and kissed her, kissed her for what seemed to be a very long time but no one, except me, appeared to take any notice.

Look! I whispered to Albert. Look!

O! that's all right. You'll get used to that, he replied negligently.

Now the kiss was over and the two began to talk, very excitedly and rapidly, as French people are wont to talk. Then, impulsively, they rose from their chairs. The man threw a coin down on his napkin. I caught the glint of gold. He gathered his arms about the woman, a lovely pale blue creature, with torrid orange hair and a hat abloom with striated petunias. They were in the middle of the street when the waiter appeared, bearing a tray, laden with plates of sliced cucumbers, radishes and butter, and tiny crayfish, and a bottle of white wine. He stared in mute astonishment at the empty table, and then picked up the coin. Finally, he glanced towards the street and, observing the retreating pair, called after them:

Mais vous n'avez pas diné!

The man turned and shot his reply over his shoulder, Nous rentrons!

The crowd on the terrasse shrieked with delight. They applauded. Some even tossed flowers from the tables after the happy couple and we. . . we sat down in the chairs they had relinquished. I am not certain that we did not eat the dinner they had ordered. At any rate we began with the cucumbers and radishes and écrevisses and a bottle of Graves Supérior.

That night in Paris I saw no Americans, at least no one seemed to be an American, and I heard no English spoken. How this came about I have no idea because it never occurred again. In fact, one meets more Americans in Paris than one does in New York and most of the French that I manage to speak I have picked up on the Island of Manhattan. During dinner I began to suspect a man without a beard, in a far corner, but Albert reassured me.

He is surely French, he said, because he is buttering his radishes.

It would be difficult to exaggerate my emotion: the white wine, the bearded French students, the exquisite women, all young and smiling and gay, all organdie and lace and sweet-peas, went to my head. I have spent many happy evenings in the Café d'Harcourt since that night. I have been there with Olive Fremstad, when she told me how, dressed as a serpent in bespangled Nile green, she had sung the finale of Salome to Edward VII in London, and one memorable Mardi-Gras night with Jane Noria, when, in a long raincoat which covered me from head to foot, standing on our table from time to time, I shouted, C'est l'heure fatale! and made as if to throw the raincoat aside but Noria, as if dreading the exposure, always dragged me down from the table, crying, No! No! until the carnival crowd, consumed with curiosity, pulled me into a corner, tore the raincoat away, and everything else too! There was another night, before the Bal des Quat'z Arts, when the café was filled with students and models in costume, and costume for the Quat'z Arts in those days, whatever it may be now, did not require the cutting out of many handkerchiefs. But the first night was the best and every other night a more or less pale reflection of that, always, indeed, coloured a little by the memory of it. So that today, when sometimes I am asked what café I prefer in Paris and I reply, the d'Harcourt, there are those who look at me a little pityingly and some even go so far as to exclaimed, O! that! but I know why it is my favourite.

Even a leisurely dinner ends at last, and I knew, as we sipped our coffee and green chartreuse and smoked our cigarettes, that this one must be over. After paying our very moderate addition, we strolled slowly away, to hop into an empty fiacre which stood on the corner a block down the boulevard. I lay back against the seat and gazed at the stars for a moment as the drive began through the warm, fragrant Paris air, the drive back to the right bank, this time across the Pont Neuf, down the Rue de Rivoli, through the Place de la Concorde, where the fountains were playing, and up the Champs-Elysées. The aroma of the chestnuts, the melting grey of the buildings, the legions of carriages and buses, filled with happy, chattering people, the glitter of electricity, all the mystic wonder of this enchanting night will always stay with me.

We drove to the Théâtre Marigny where we saw a revue; at least we were present at a revue; I do not remember to have seen or heard anything on the stage. Between the acts, we walked in the open foyer, at this theatre a sort of garden, and admired the cocottes, great ladies of some distant epoch, they seemed to me, in their toilets from Redfern and Doucet and Chéruit and Callot Sœurs, their hats from the Rue de la Paix and the Place Vendôme, their exceedingly elaborate and decoratively artificial complexions. Later, we sipped cassis on the balcony. It was Spring in Paris and I was young! The chestnut trees were heavy with white blossoms and the air was laden with their perfume. I gazed down the Champs-Elysées, surely the true Elysian Fields, a myriad of lights shining through the dark green, the black, leaved branches. I do not think I spoke many words and I know that Albert did not. He may have been bored, but I think he derived some slight pleasure from my juvenile enthusiasm for, although Paris was old hat to him, he loved this particular old hat.

We must have stopped somewhere for more drinks on the way home, perhaps at Weber's in the Rue Royale, where there was a gipsy band. I do not remember, but I am sure that it was nearly four in the morning when we drove up before the little hotel in the Place de l'Odéon and when, after we had paid the driver and dismissed him, I discovered to my astonishment that the door was locked. Albert assured me that this was the custom and that I must ring for the concierge. So I pulled the knob, and even outside we could hear the distant reverberations of the bell, but no reply came, and the door remained closed. It was Joseph's job to open the door and Joseph was asleep and refused to awaken. Again and again we pulled the cord, the bell tinkling in the vast silence, for the street was utterly deserted, but still no one came. At last we desisted, Albert suggesting that I go home with him. We walked a few paces until we came to the iron fence surrounding the Luxembourg Gardens and there, lying beside it, I espied a ladder, left by some negligent workman.

But my room is on the first floor. The window is open; it looks over the Place. I can enter with the ladder, I cried.

Albert, amused, helped me carry it back. Set up, it just reached the window and I swiftly scaled it and clambered into the room, waving my hand back to Albert, who hoisted the ladder to his shoulder as he started up the street trying to whistle, Viens Poupoule! but laughing to himself all the time, so that the tune cracked. As for me, I lighted one of my candles, undressed, threw the feather-bed off to the floor, and climbed into bed. Then I blew out the candle and soon fell asleep. It was the tenth of May, 1907, that I spent my first night in Paris.

II

It must have been nearly noon when I awakened and drew back the heavy curtains to let the sunlight into my room, as I have since seen so many French actresses do on the stage. I rang the bell, and when Joseph appeared, I asked for hot water, chocolate and rolls. Presently, he returned with a little can of tepid water and my breakfast on a tray. While I sponged myself, I listened to the cacophony of the street, the boys calling vegetables, the heavy rumbling of the buses on the rough pavement, the shrieking and tooting of the automobile sirens. Then I sipped my chocolate and munched my croissant, feeling very happy. My past had dropped from me like a crustacean's discarded shell. I was in Paris and it still seemed possible to live in Paris as I had been told that one lived there. It was exactly like the books.

After my breakfast, I dressed slowly, and wandered out, past the peristyle of the Odéon, where I afterwards spent so many contented hours searching for old plays, on through the now open gate of the Luxembourg Gardens, gaily sprinkled with children and their nounous, students and sweet girls, charming old ladies with lace caps on their heads and lace scarfs round their shoulders, and painters, working away at their canvases on easels. In the pool in front of the Senate, boys were launching their toy sloops and schooners and, a little further away on the gravel walk, other boys were engaged in the more active sport of diabolo. The gardens were ablaze with flowers but a classic order was maintained for which the stately rows of clipped limes furnished the leading note. The place seemed to have been created for pleasure. Even the dingy statues of the queens smiled at me. I sat on a bench, dreaming, until an old crone approached and asked me for a sou. I thought her a beggar until she returned the change from a fifty centimes piece which I had given her, explaining that one sou was the price of my seat. There were free seats too, I discovered after I had paid.

The Luxembourg Gardens have always retained their hold over my imagination. I never visit Paris without spending several hours there, sometimes in the bright morning light, sometimes in the late afternoon, when the military band plays dolent tunes, usually by Massenet, sometimes a spectator at one of the guignols and, very often in the autumn, when the leaves are falling, I sit silently on a bench before the Medici fountain, entirely unconscious of the passing of time. The Luxembourg

Gardens always envelop me in a sentimental mood. Their atmosphere is softly poetic, old-fashioned, melancholy. I am near to tears now, merely thinking of them, and I am sure the tears came to my eyes even on that bright May morning fourteen years ago.

Did I, attracted by the strange name, lunch at the Deux-Magots? It is possible. I know that later I strolled down the Rue de Seine and along the quais, examining eighteenth century books, buying old numbers of l'Assiette au Beurre, and talking with the quaint vendors, most of them old men. Then I wandered up the Rue de Richelieu, studying the examples of fine bindings in the windows of the shops on either hand. About three o'clock, I mounted the impériale of a bus, not even asking where it was going. I didn't care. I descended before the gate of the Parc Monceau and passed a few happy moments in the presence of the marble lady in a dress of the nineties, who reads Guy de Maupassant in the shadow of his bust, and a few more by the Naumachie, the oval pool, flanked by a semi-circular Corinthian colonnade in a state of picturesque ruin.

At a quarter before four, I left the parc and, hailing a fiacre, bade the driver take me to Martha Baker's studio in the Avenue Victor Hugo, where I had an appointment. Martha was painting my portrait. She had begun work on the picture in Chicago the year before but when I went to New York, she went to Paris. So it was still unfinished and I had promised to come to her for more sittings. Now, in Chicago, Martha noted that I grew restless on the model stand and she had found it expedient to ask people in to talk to me, so that my face would not become dead and sullen. There, I usually knew the people she would ask, but it occurred to me, as I was driving to her door, that in Paris I knew no one, so that, if she followed her habit, I would see new faces.

The cocher stopped his horse before an old stone house and I entered. Challenged by the concierge, I asked for Mademoiselle Bahker, and was directed to go through the courtyard into a back passageway, up the stairs, where I would find Mademoiselle Bahker, troisième à gauche. I followed these instructions and knocked at the door. Martha, herself, opened it.

Oh, Carl, it's you! I'm so glad to see you!

Martha had not changed. She and even her studio were much as they had been in Chicago. She is dead now, dead possibly of a broken heart; certainly she was never happy. Her Insouciance, the portrait of Elizabeth Buehrmann, in a green cloth dress trimmed with fur, and a miniature or two hang in the Art Institute in Chicago, but during her lifetime she never received the kind of appreciation she really craved. She had an uncanny talent for portraiture, a talent which in some respects I have never seen equalled by any of her coevals. Artists, as a matter of fact, generally either envied or admired her. Her peculiar form of genius lay in the facility with which she caught her sitters' weaknesses. Possibly this is the reason she did not sell more pictures, for her models were frequently dissatisfied. It was exasperating, doubtless, to find oneself caught in paint on canvas against an unenviable immortality. Her sitters were exposed, so to speak; petty vices shone forth; Martha almost idealized the faults of her subjects. It would be impossible for the model to strut or pose before one of her pictures. It told the truth. Sargent caught the trick once. I have been informed that a physician diagnosed the malady of an American lady, his patient, after studying Sargent's portrait of her.

Martha should have painted our presidents, our mayors, our politicians, our authors, our college presidents, and our critics. Posterity might have learned more from such portraits than from volumes of psychoanalytic biography. But most of her sitters were silly Chicago ladies, not particularly weak because they were not particularly strong. On the few occasions on which in her capacity as an artist she had faced character, her brushes unerringly depicted something beneath the surface. She tore away men's masks and, with a kind of mystic understanding, painted their insides. How it was done, I don't know. Probably she herself didn't know. Many an artist is ignorant of the secret of his own method. If I had ascribed this quality to Martha during her lifetime, which I never did, she might not have taken it as praise. It may not, indeed, have been her ambition, although truth was undoubtedly her ambition. Speculation aside, this was no art for Chicago. I doubt, indeed, if it would have been popular anywhere, for men the world over are alike in this, that they not only prefer to be painted in masks, they even want the artist to flatter the mask a bit.

The studio, I observed at once, was a little arty, a little more arty than a painter's studio usually is. It was arranged, of that there could be no doubt. There were, to be sure, canvases stacked against the wall in addition to those which were hanging, but they had been stacked with a crafty hand, one indubious of its effect. For the rest, the tables and couches were strewn with brocades and laces, and lilacs and mimosa bloomed in brown and blue and green earthenware bowls on the tables.

Later, I knew that marigolds and zinnias would replace these and, later still, violets and gardenias. On an easel stood my unfinished portrait and a palette and a box of paints lay on a stool nearby.

Martha herself wore a soft, clinging, dark-green woolen dress, almost completely covered by a brown denim painter's blouse. Her hair was her great glory, long, reddish gold Mélisande hair which, when uncoiled, hung far below her knees, but today it was knotted loosely on top of her head. Her face, keen and searching, wore an expression that might be described as wistful; discontent lurked somewhere between her eyes and her mouth. Her complexion was sallow and she wore eyeglasses.

There was some one else present, a girl, sitting in a shadowy corner, who rose as I entered. A strong odour of Cœur de Jeannette hovered about her. She was an American. She was immediately introduced as Miss Clara Barnes of Chicago, but I would have known she was an American had she not been so introduced. She wore a shirt-waist and skirt. She had very black hair, parted in the middle, a face that it would have been impossible to remember ten minutes and which now, although I have seen her many times since, I have completely forgotten, and very thick ankles. I gathered presently that she was in Paris to study singing as were so many girls like her. Very soon, I sized her up as the kind of girl who thinks that antimacassars are ottomans, that tripe is a variety of fish, that Così Fan Tutte is an Italian ice cream, that the pope's nose is a nasal appendage which has been blessed by the head of the established church, that The Beast in the Jungle is an animal story, and that when one says Arthur Machen one means Harry Mencken.

Well, we'd best begin, said Martha. It's late.

Isn't it *too* late? I was rather surprised when you asked me to come in the afternoon.

Martha smiled but there was a touch of petulance in her reply: I knew you wouldn't get up very early the morning after your first night in Paris, and I knew if I didn't get you here today there would be small chance of getting you here at all. If you come again, of course it will be in the morning.

I climbed to the model chair, seated myself, grasped the green book that was part of the composition, and automatically assumed that woebegone expression that is worn by all amateurs who pose for their portraits.

That won't do at all, said Martha. I asked Clara to come here to amuse you.

Clara tried. She told me that she was studying Manon and that she had been to the Opéra-Comique fifteen times to hear the opera.

Garden is all wrong in it, all wrong, she continued. In the first place she can't sing. Of course she's pretty, but she's not my idea of Manon at all. I will really *sing* the part and act it too.

A month or two later, while we munched sandwiches and drank beer between the acts of Tristan und Isolde in the foyer of the Prinzregenten Theater in Munich, Olive Fremstad introduced me to an American girl, who informed me that a new Isolde had been born that day.

I shall be the great Isolde, she remarked casually, and her name, I gathered, when I asked Madame Fremstad to repeat it, was Minnie Saltzmann-Stevens.

But on the day that Clara spoke of her future triumphs in Manon, I had yet to become accustomed to this confidence with which beginners in the vocal art seem so richly endowed, a confidence which is frequently disturbed by circumstances for, as George Moore has somewhere said, our dreams and our circumstances are often in conflict. Later, I discovered that every unsuccessful singer believes, and asserts, that Geraldine Farrar is instrumental in preventing her from singing at the Metropolitan Opera House. On this day, I say, I was unaware of this peculiarity in vocalists but I was interested in the name she had let slip, a name I had never before heard.

Who is Garden? I asked.

You don't know Mary Garden! exclaimed Martha.

There! shrieked Clara. There! I told you so. No one outside of Paris has ever even heard of the woman.

Well, they've heard of her here, said Martha, quietly, pinching a little worm of cobalt blue from a tube. She's the favourite singer of the Opéra-Comique. She is an American and she sings Louise and Manon and Traviata and Mélisande and Aphrodite, especially Aphrodite.

She's singing Aphrodite tonight, said Miss Barnes.

And what is she like? I queried.

Well, Clara began dubiously, she is said to be like Sybil Sanderson but, of course, Sanderson had a voice and, she hurried on, you know even Sanderson never had any success in New York.

I recalled, only too readily, how Manon with Jean de Reszke, Pol Plançon, and Sybil Sanderson in the cast had failed in the nineties at the Metropolitan Opera House, and I admitted as much to Clara.

But would this be true today? I pondered.

Certainly, advanced Clara. America doesn't want French singers. They never know how to sing.

But you are studying in Paris.

The girl began to look discomfited.

With an Italian teacher, she asseverated.

It delighted me to be able to add, I think Sanderson studied with Sbriglia and Madame Marchesi.

Your face is getting very hard, cried Martha in despair.

I think he is very rude, exclaimed the outraged and contumacious Miss Barnes, with a kind of leering acidity. He doesn't seem to know the difference between tradition and impertinent improvisation. He doesn't see that singing at the Opéra or the Opéra-Comique with a lot of rotten French singers would ruin anybody who didn't have training enough to stand out against this influence, singing utterly un-musical parts like Mélisande, too, parlando rôles calculated to ruin any voice. Maeterlinck won't even go to hear the opera, it's so rotten. I wonder how much Mr. Van Vechten knows about music anyway?

Very little, I remarked mildly.

O! wailed Martha, you're not entertaining Carl at all and I can't paint when you squabble. Carl's very nice. Why can't you be agreeable, Clara? What is the matter?

Miss Barnes disdained to reply. She drew herself into a sort of sulk, crossing her thick ankles massively. The scent of Cœur de Jeannette seemed to grow heavier. Within bounds, I was amused by her display of emotion but I was also bored. My face must have showed it. Martha worked on for a moment or two and then flung down her brushes.

It's no good, no good at all, she announced. You have no expression today. I can't get behind your mask. Your face is completely empty.

And, I may add, as this was the last day that Martha ever painted on this portrait, she never did get behind the mask. To that extent I triumphed, and the picture still exists to confuse people as to my real personality. It is as empty as if it had been painted by Boldini or McEvoy. Fortunately for her future reputation in this regard, Martha had already painted a portrait of me which is sufficiently revealing.

I must have stretched and yawned at this point, for Martha looked cross, when a welcome interruption occurred in the form of a knock at the door. Martha walked across the room. As she opened the door, directly opposite where I was sitting, I saw the slender figure of a young man, perhaps twenty-one years old. He was carefully dressed in a light grey suit with a herring-bone pattern, and wore a neck-scarf of deep blue. He carried a stick and buckskin gloves in one hand and a straw hat in the other.

Why, it's Peter! cried Martha. I wish you had come sooner.

This is Peter Whiffle, she said, leading him into the room and then, as he extended his hand to me, You know Clara Barnes.

He turned away to bow but I had already caught his interesting face, his deep blue eyes that shifted rather uneasily but at the same time remained honest and frank, his clear, simple expression, his high brow, his curly, blue-black hair, carefully parted down the centre of his head. He spoke to me at once.

Martha has said a good deal, perhaps too much about you. Still, I have wanted to meet you.

You must tell me who you are, I replied.

I should have told you, only you just arrived, Martha put in. I had no idea that Peter would come in today. He is the American Flaubert or Anatole France or something. He is writing a book. What *is* your book about, Peter?

Whiffle smiled, drew out a cigarette-case of Toledo work, extracted a cigarette from it, and said, I haven't the slightest idea. Then, as if he thought this might be construed as rudeness, or false modesty, or a rather viscous attempt at secrecy, he added, I really haven't, not the remotest. I want to talk to you about it. . . That's why I wanted to meet you. Martha says that you know. . . well, that you *know*.

You really should be painting Mr. Van Vechten now, said Clara Barnes, with a trace of malice. He has the right expression.

I hope I haven't interrupted your work, said Peter.

No, I'm through today, Martha rejoined. We're neither of us in the mood. Besides it's absurd to try to paint in this light.

Painting, Peter went on, is not any easier than writing. Always the search for—for what? he asked suddenly, turning to me.

For truth, I suppose, I replied.

I thought you would say that but that's not what I meant, that's not at all what I meant.

This logograph rather concluded that subject, for Peter did not explain what it was that he did mean. Neither did he wear a conscious air of obfuscation. He rambled on about many things, spoke of new people, new books, new music, and he also mentioned Mary Garden.

I have heard of Mary Garden for the first time today, I said, and I am beginning to be interested.

You haven't seen her? demanded Peter. But she is stupendous, soul, body, imagination, intellect, everything! How few there are. A lyric Mélisande, a caressing Manon, a throbbingly wicked Chrysis. She is the cult in Paris and the Opéra-Comique is the Temple where she is worshipped. I think some day this new religion will be carried to America. He stopped. Let me see, what am I doing tonight? O! yes, I know. I won't do that. Will you go with me to hear Aphrodite?

Of course, I will. I have just come to Paris and I want to do and hear and see everything.

Well, we'll go, he announced, but I noted that his tone was curiously indecisive. We'll go to dinner first.

You're not going to dinner yet? Martha demanded rather querulously.

Not quite yet. Then, turning to Clara, How's the Voice?

It was my first intimation that Clara had thus symbolized her talent in the third person. People were not expected to refer to her as Clara or Miss Barnes; she was the Voice.

The Voice is doing very well indeed, Clara, now quite mollified, rejoined. I'm studying Manon, and if you like Mary Garden, wait until you hear me!

Peter continued to manipulate Clara with the proper address. The conversation bubbled or languished, I forget which; at any rate, a half hour or so later, Peter and I were seated in a taxi-cab, bound for Foyot's where he had decided we would dine; at least I thought he had decided, but soon he seemed doubtful.

Foyot's, Foyot's, he rolled the name meditatively over on his tongue. I don't know. . .

We leaned back against the seat and drank in the soft air. I don't think that we talked very much. The cocher was driving over the bridge of Alexandre III with its golden horses gleaming in the late afternoon sunlight when Peter bent forward and addressed him,

Allez au Café Anglais.

Where meant nothing to me, but I was a little surprised at his hesitation. The cocher changed his route, grumbling a bit, for he was out of his course.

I don't know why I ever suggested Foyot, said Peter, or the Café Anglais either. We'll go to the Petit Riche.

III

I f the reader has been led to expect a chapter devoted to an account of Mary Garden in Aphrodite, he will be disappointed. I did not see Mary Garden that evening, nor for many evenings thereafter, and I do not remember, indeed, that Peter Whiffle ever referred to her again. We dined at a quiet little restaurant, Boilaive by name, near the Folies-Bergère. The interior, as bare of decoration as are most such interiors in Paris, where the food and wines are given more consideration than the mural paintings, was no larger than that of a small shop. My companion led me straight to a tiny winding staircase in one corner, which we ascended, and presently we found ourselves in a private room, with three tables in it, to be sure, but two of these remained unoccupied. We began our dinner with escargots à la bordelaise, which I was eating for the first time, but I have never been squeamish about novel food. A man with a broad taste in food is inclined to be tolerant in regard to everything. Also, when he begins to understand the cooking of a nation, he is on the way to an understanding of the nation itself. There were many other dishes, but I particularly remember a navarin because Peter spoke of it, pointing out that every country has one dish in which it is honourable to put whatever is left over in the larder. In China (or out of it, in Chinese restaurants), this dish is called chop suey; in Ireland, Irish stew; in Spain, olla or puchero; in France, ragoût or navarin; in Italy, minestra; and in America, hash. We lingered over such matters, getting acquainted, so to speak, passing through the polite stages of early conversation, slipping beyond the poses that one unconsciously assumes with a new friend. I think I did most of the talking, although Whiffle told me that he had come from Ohio, that he was in Paris on a sort of mission, something to do with literature, I gathered. We ate and drank slowly and it must have been nearly ten when he paid the bill and we drove away, this time to Fouquet's, an open-air restaurant in the Champs-Elysées, where we sat on the broad terrasse and drank many bocks, so many, indeed, that by the time we had decided to settle our account, the saucers in front of us were piled almost to our chins. We should probably have remained there all night, had he not suggested that I go to his rooms with him. That night, my second in Paris, I would have gone anywhere with any one. But there was that in Peter Whiffle which had awakened both my interest and my curiosity for I, too, had the ambition to write, and it seemed to me possible that I was in the presence of a writing man, an author.

We entered another taxi-auto or fiacre, I don't remember and it doesn't matter, there were so many peregrinations in those days, and we drove to an apartment house in a little street near the Rue Blanche. The house being modern, there was an ascenseur and I experienced for the first time the thrill of one of those little personally conducted lifts, in which you press your own button and take your own chances. Since that night I have had many strange misadventures with these intransigent elevators, but on this occasion, miraculously, the machine stopped at the fourth floor, as it had been bidden, and soon we were in the sitting-room of Whiffle's apartment, a room which I still remember, although subsequently I have been in half a dozen of his other rooms in various localities.

It was very orderly, this room, although not exactly arranged, at any rate not arranged like Martha's studio, as if to set object against object and colour against colour. It was a neat little ivory French room, with a white fire-place, picked in gold, surmounted by a gilt clock and Louis XVI candlesticks. There were charming aquatints on the ivory walls and chairs and tables of the Empire period. The tables were laden with neat piles of pamphlets. Beside a typewriter, was ranged a heap of note-books at least a foot high and stacked on the floor in one corner there were other books, formidable looking volumes of weight and heft, "thick bulky octavos with cut-and-come-again expressions," apparently dictionaries and lexicons. An orange Persian cat lay asleep in one of the chairs as we entered, but he immediately stretched himself, extending his noble paws, yawning and arching his back, and then came forward to greet us, purring.

Hello, George! cried Whiffle, as the cat waved his magnificent red tail back and forth and rubbed himself against Peter's leg.

George? I queried.

Yes, that's George Moore. He goes everywhere with me in a basket, when I travel, and he is just as contented in Toledo as he is in Paris, anywhere there is raw meat to be had. Places mean nothing to him. My best friend.

I sat in one of the chairs and lit a cigarette. Peter brought out a bottle of cognac and a couple of glasses. He threw open the shutters and the soft late sounds of the city filtered in with the fresh spring air. One could just hear the faint tinkle of an orchestra at some distant bal.

I like you, Van Vechten, my host began at last, and I've got to talk to somebody. My work has just begun and there's so much to say about it. Tell me to stop when you get tired. . . In a way, I want to know what you think; in another way, it helps me merely to talk, in the working out of my ideas. But who was there to talk to, I mean before you came? I can see that you may be interested in what I am trying to do, good God! in what I *will* do! I've done a lot already. . .

You have begun your book then?

Well, you might say so, but I haven't written a line. I've collected the straw; the bricks will come. I've not been idle. You see those catalogues?

I nodded.

He fumbled them over. Then, without a break, with a strange glow of exhilaration on his pale ethereal face, his eyes flashing, his hands gesticulating, his body swaying, marching up and down the room, he recited with a crescendo which mounted to a magnificent fortissimo in the coda:

Perfumery catalogues: Coty, Houbigant, Atkinson, Rigaud, Rue de la Paix, Bond Street, Place Vendôme, Regent Street, Nirvana, Chypre, Sakountala, Ambre, Après l'Ondée, Quelques Fleurs, Fougère Royale, Myrbaha, Yavahnah, Gaudika, Délices de Péra, Cœur de Jeannette, Djer Kiss, Jockey-Club, and the Egyptian perfumes, Myrrh and Kyphy. Did you know that Richelieu lived in an atmosphere heavily laden with the most pungent perfumes to inflame his sexual imagination? Automobile catalogues: Mercedes, Rolls-Royce, Ford, tires, self-starters, limousines, carburettors, gas. Jewellery catalogues: heaps of 'em, all about diamonds and platinum, chrysoprase and jade, malachite and chalcedony, amethysts and garnets, and the emerald, the precious stone which comes the nearest to approximating that human manifestation known as art, because it always has flaws; red jasper, sacred to the rosy god, Bacchus, the green plasma, blood-stone, cornelian, cat's-eye, amber, with its medicinal properties, the Indian jewels, spinels, the reddish orange jacinth, and the violet almandine. Did you know that the Emperor Claudius used to clothe himself in smaragds and sardonyx stones and that Pope Paul II died of a cold caught from the weight and chill of the rings which loaded his aged fingers? Are you aware that the star-topaz is as rare as a Keutschacher Rubentaler of the year 1504? Yonder is a volume which treats of the glyptic lore. In it you may read of the Assyrian cylinders fashioned from red and green serpentine, the Egyptian scarabei, carved in steaschist;

you may learn of the seal-cutters of Nineveh and of the Signet of Sennacherib, now preserved in the British Museum. Do you know that a jewel engraved with Hercules at the fountain was deposited in the tomb of the Frankish King Childeric at Tournay? Do you know of Mnesarchus, the Tyrrhene gem cutter, who practised his art at Samos? Have you seen the Julia of Evodus, engraved in a giant aquamarine, or the Byzantine topaz, carved with the figure of the blind bow-boy, sacrificing the Psyche-butterfly, or the emerald signet of Polycrates, with the lyre cut upon it, or the Etruscan peridot representing a sphinx scratching her ear with her hind paw, or the sapphire, discovered in a disused well at Hereford, in which the head of the Madonna has been chiseled, with the inscription, round the beasil, in Lombard letters, TECTA LEGE LECTA TEGE, or the jacinth engraved with the triple face of Baphomet, with a legend of darkly obscene purport? The breastplate of the Jewish High Priest had its oracular gems, which were the Urim and Thummim. Apollonius Tyaneus, the sorcerer, for the purposes of his enchantments, wore special rings with appropriate stones for each day of the week. Also, in this curious book, and others which you may examine, such as George III's Dactyliotheca Smithiana (Venice; 1767), you will find some account of the gems of the Gnostics; an intaglio in a pale convex plasma, carved with the Chnuphis Serpent, raising himself aloft, with the seven vowels, the elements of his name, above; another jewel engraved with the figure of the jackal-headed Anubis, the serpent with the lion's head, the infant Horus, seated on the lotus, the cynocephalus baboon, and the Abraxas-god, Iao, created from the four elements; an Egyptian seal of the god, Harpocrates, seated on the mystic lotus, in adoration of the Yoni; and an esoteric green jasper amulet in the form of a dragon, surrounded by rays. Florists' catalogues: strangely wicked cyclamens, meat-eating begonias, beloved of des Esseintes (Henri Matisse grows these peccant plants in his garden and they suggest his work), shaggy chrysanthemums, orchids, green, white, and mauve, the veined salpiglossis, the mournful, rich-smelling tube-rose, all the mystic blossoms adored by Robert de la Condamine's primitive, tortured, orgiastic saints in The Double Garden, marigolds and daisies, the most complex and the most simple flowers of all, hypocritical fuchsias, and calceolaria, sacred to la bella Cenerentola. Reaper catalogues: you know, the McCormicks and the Middle West. Porcelain catalogues: Rookwood, Royal Doulton, Wedgwood, Delft, the quaint, clean, heavy, charming Brittany ware, Majolica, the wondrous Chinese porcelains, self-colour, sang de bœuf, apple of roses, peach-blow, Sèvres, signed with the fox of Emile Renard, or the eye of Pajou, or the little house of Jean-Jacques Anteaume. Furniture catalogues: Adam and Louis XV, Futurist, Empire, Venetian and Chinese, Poincaré and Grand Rapids. Artdealers' catalogues: Félicien Rops and Jo Davidson, Renoir and Franz Hals, Cranach and Picasso, Manet and Carpaccio. Book-dealers' catalogues: George Borrow, Thomas Love Peacock, Ambrose Bierce, William Beckford, Robert Smith Surtees, Francis William Bain. Do you know the true story of Ambrose Gwinett, related by Oliver Goldsmith: the fellow who, having been hanged and gibbeted for murdering a traveller with whom he had shared his bed-chamber at a tavern, revived in the night, shipped at sea as a sailor, and later met on a vessel the man for whose murder he had been hung? Gwinett's supposed victim had been attacked during the night with a severe bleeding of the nose, had risen and left the house for a walk by the sea-wall, and had been shanghaied. Catalogues of curious varieties of cats: Australian, with long noses and long hind-legs, like kangaroos, Manx cats without any tails and chocolate and fawn Siamese cats with sapphire eyes, the cacodorous Russian blue cats, and male tortoise-shells. Catalogues of tinshops: tin plates, tin cups, and can openers. Catalogues of laces: Valenciennes and Cluny and Chantilly and double-knot, Punto in Aria, a Spanish lace of the sixteenth century, lace constructed of human hair or aloe fibre, Point d'Espagne, made by Jewesses. Catalogues of toys: an engine that spreads smoke in the air, as it runs around a track with a circumference of eight feet, a doll that cries, Uncle! Uncle! a child's opium set. Catalogues of operas: Marta and Don Pasquale, Der Freischütz and Mefistofele, Simon Bocanegra and La Dolores. Cook-Books: Mrs. Pennell's The Feasts of Autolycus, a grandiose treatise on the noblest of the arts, wherein you may read of the amorous adventures of The Triumphant Tomato and the Incomparable Onion, Mr. Finck's Food and Flavour, the gentle Abraham Hayward on The Art of Dining, the biography of Vatel, the super-cook who killed himself because the fish for the king's dinner were missing, Mrs. Glasse's Cookery, which Dr. Johnson boasted that he could surpass, and, above all, Jean Anthelme Brillat-Savarin's Physiologie du Goût. Catalogues of harness, bits and saddles. Catalogues of cigarettes: Dimitrinos and Melachrinos, Fatimas and Sweet Caporals. Catalogues of liqueurs: Danziger Goldwasser and Crème Yvette, Parfait Amour, as tanagrine as the blood in the sacred altar chalice. Catalogues of paints: yellow ochre and gamboge, burnt sienna and Chinese vermilion. Catalogues of hats: derbies and fedoras, straw and felt hats, top-hats and caps, sombreros, tam-o'shanters, billycocks, shakos and tarbooshes. . .

He stopped, breathless with excitement, demanding, What do you think of that?

I don't know what to think. . .

I'm sure you don't. That isn't all. There are dictionaries and lexicons, not only German, English, French, Italian, Russian, and Spanish, but also Hebrew, Persian, Magyar, Chinese, Zend, Sanscrit, Hindustani, Negro dialects, French argot, Portuguese, American slang, and Pennsylvania Dutch.

And what are those curious pamphlets?

He lifted a few and read off the titles:

A study of the brain of the late Major J. W. Powell.

A study of the anatomic relations of the optic nerve to the accessory cavities of the nose.

On regeneration in the pigmented skin of the frog and on the character of the chromatophores.

The chondrocranium of an embryo pig.

Morphology of the parthogenetic development of amphitrite.

Note on the influence of castration on the weight of the brain and spinal cord in the albino rat.

There are, he added solemnly, many strange words in these pamphlets, not readily to be found elsewhere.

Now Peter pointed to the pile of note-books on the table.

These are my note-books. I have ranged Paris for my material. For days I have walked in the Passage des Panoramas and the Rue St. Honoré, making lists of every object in the windows. In the case of books I have described the bindings. I have stopped before the shops of fruit vendors, antique dealers, undertakers, jewellers, and fashioners of artificial flowers. I have spent so much time in the Galeries Lafayette and the Bon Marché that I have probably been mistaken for a shoplifter. These books are full of results. What do you think of it?

But what is all this for?

For my work, of course. For my work.

I can't imagine, I began almost in a whisper, I was so astonished, what you do, what you are going to do. Are you writing an encyclopedia?

No, my intention is not to define or describe, but to enumerate. Life is made up of a collection of objects, and the mere citation of them is sufficient to give the reader a sense of form and colour, atmosphere and *style*. And form, style, manner in literature are everything; subject is nothing. Nothing whatever, he added impressively, after a pause. Do you know what Buffon wrote: Style is the only passport to posterity. It is not range of information, nor mastery of some little known branch of science, nor yet novelty of matter, that will insure immortality. Recall the great writers, Théophile Gautier, Jules Barbey d'Aurevilly, Joris Huysmans, Oscar Wilde: they all used this method, catalogues, catalogues, catalogues! All great art is a matter of cataloguing life, summing it up in a list of objects. This is so true that the commercial catalogues themselves are almost works of art. Their only flaw is that they pause to describe. If it only listed objects, without defining them, a dealer's catalogue would be as precious as a book by Gautier.

During this discourse, George Moore, the orange cat, had been wandering around, rather restlessly, occasionally gazing at Peter with a semi-quizzical expression and an absurd cock of the ears. At some point or other, however, he had evidently arrived at the conclusion that this extra display of emotion on the part of his human companion boded him no evil and, having satisfied himself in this regard, he leaped lightly to the mantelshelf, circled his enormous bulk miraculously around three or four times on the limited space at his disposal, and sank into a profound slumber when, probably, with dreams of garrets full of lazy mice, his ears and his tail, which depended a foot below the shelf, began to twitch.

Peter continued to talk: d'Aurevilly wrote his books in different coloured inks. It was a wonderful idea. Black ink would never do to describe certain scenes, certain objects. I can imagine an entire book written in purple, or green, or blood-red, but the best book would be written in many colours. Consider, for a moment, the distinction between purple and violet, shades which are cousins: the one suggests the most violent passions or something royal or papal, the other a nunnery or a widow, or a being bereft of any capacity for passion.

Henry James should write his books in white ink on white paper and, by a system of analogy, you can very well see that Rider Haggard should write his books in white ink on black paper. Pale ideas, obviously expressed. Gold! Think what you could do with gold! If silence is golden, surely the periods, the commas, the semicolons, and dashes should be of gold. But not only the stops could gleam and shine; whole silent pages might glitter. And blue, bright blue; what more suggestive colour for the writer than bright blue?

Not only should manuscripts be written in multi-coloured inks, but they should be written on multi-coloured papers, and then they should be printed in multi-coloured inks on multi-coloured papers. The art of book-making, in the sense that the making of a book is part of its authorship, part of its creation, is not even begun.

The sculptor is not satisfied with moulding his idea in clay; he gives it final form in marble or malachite or jade or bronze. Many an author, however, having completed work on his manuscript, is content to allow his publisher to choose the paper, the ink, the binding, the typography: all, obviously, part of the author's task. It is the publisher's wish, no doubt, to issue the book as cheaply as possible, and to this end he will make as many books after the same model as he practicably can. But every book should have a different appearance from every other book. Every book should have the aspect to which its ideas give birth. The form of the material should dictate the form of the binding. Who but a fool, for example, would print and bind Lavengro and Roderick Hudson in a similar manner? And yet that is just what publishers will do if they are let alone.

Peter had become so excited that he had awakened George Moore, who now descended from the mantelpiece and sought the seclusion of a couch in the corner where, after a few abortive licks at his left hind-leg, and a pretence of scrubbing his ears, he again settled into sleep. As for me, I listened, entranced, and as the night before I had discovered Paris, it seemed to me now that I was discovering the secrets of the writer's craft and I determined to go forth in the morning with a note-book, jotting down the names of every object I encountered.

I must have been somewhat bewildered for I repeated a question I had asked before:

Have you written anything yet?

Not yet. . . I am collecting my materials. It may take me considerably longer to collect what I shall require for a very short book.

What is the book to be about?

Van Vechten, Van Vechten, you are not following me! he cried, and he again began to walk up and down the little room. What is the book to be about? Why, it is to be about the names of the things I have collected. It is to be about three hundred pages, he added triumphantly.

That is what it is to be about, about three hundred pages, three hundred pages of colour and style and lists, lists of objects, all jumbled artfully. There isn't a moral, or an idea, or a plot, or even a character. There's to be no propaganda or preaching, or violence, or emotion, or even humour. I am not trying to imitate Dickens or Dostoevsky. They did not write books; they wrote newspapers. Art eliminates all such rubbish. Art has nothing to do with ideas. Art is abstract. When art becomes concrete it is no longer art. Thank God, I know what I want to do! Thank God, I haven't wasted my time admiring hack work! Thank God, I can start in at once constructing a masterpiece! Why a list of passengers sailing on the Kronprinz Wilhelm is more nearly a work of art than a novel by Thomas Hardy! What is there in that? Anybody can do it. Where is the arrangement, the colour, the form? Hardy merely photographs life!

But aren't you trying to photograph still life?

Peter's face was almost purple; I thought he would burst a blood-vessel.

Don't you understand that perfumes and reaping-machines are never to be found together in real life? That is art, making a pattern, dragging unfamiliar words and colours and sounds together until they form a pattern, a beautiful pattern. An Aubusson carpet is art, and it is assuredly not a photograph of still life. . . Art. . .

I don't know how much more of this there was but, when Peter finally stopped talking, the sunlight was streaming in through the window.

IV

It was many days before I saw Peter again. I met other men and women. I visited the Louvre and at first stood humbly in the Salon Carré before the Monna Lisa and in the long corridor of the Venus de Milo; a little later, I became thuriferous before Sandro Botticelli's frescoes from the Villa Lemmi and Watteau's Pierrot. I made a pilgrimage to the Luxembourg Gallery and read Huysmans's evocation of the picture before Moreau's Salome. I sat in the tiny old Roman arena, Lutetia's amphitheatre, constructed in the second or third century, and conjured up visions of lions and Christian virgins. I drank tea at the Pavillon. d'Armenonville in the Bois and I bought silk handkerchiefs of many colours at the Galeries Lafayette. I began to carry my small change in a pig-skin purse and I learned to look out for bad money. Every morning I called for mail at the American Express Company in the Rue Scribe. I ate little wild strawberries with Crème d'Isigny. I bought old copies of l'Assiette au Beurre on the quais and new copies of Le Sourire at kiosques. I heard Werther at the Opéra-Comique and I saw Lina Cavalieri in Thaïs at the Opéra. I made journeys to Versailles, Saint Cloud, and Fontainebleau. I inspected the little hotel in the Rue des Beaux-Arts where Oscar Wilde died and I paid my respects to his tomb in Père-Lachaise. The fig-leaf was missing from the heroic figure on the monument. It had been stolen, the cemetery-guard informed me, par une jeune miss anglaise, who desired a souvenir. I drank champagne cocktails, sitting on a stool, at the American bar in the Grand Hotel. I drank whisky and soda, ate salted nuts, and talked with English racing men at Henry's bar, under the delightful brown and yellow mural decorations, exploiting ladies of the 1880 period with bangs, and dresses with bustles, and over drapings, and buttons down the front. I enjoyed long bus rides and I purchased plays in the arcades of the Odéon. I went to the races at Chantilly. I drank cocktails at Louis's bar in the Rue Racine. Louis Doerr, the patron, had worked as a bar-man in Chicago and understood the secrets of American mixed drinks. Doubtless, he could have made a Fireman's Shirt. He divided his time between his little bar and his atelier, where he gave boxing lessons to the students of the quarter. When he was teaching the manly art, Madame Doerr manipulated the shaker. I attended services at Les Hannetons and Maurice's Bar and I strolled through the Musée de Cluny, where

CARL VAN VECHTEN

I bought postcards of chastity belts and instruments of torture. I read Maupassant in the Parc Monceau. I took in the naughty revues at Parisiana, the Ba-ta-clan, and the Folies-Bergère. I purchased many English and American novels in the Tauchnitz edition and I discovered a miniature shop in the Rue de Furstenberg, where elegant reprints of bawdy eighteenth century French romances might be procured. I climbed to the top of the towers of Notre-Dame, particularly to observe a chimère which was said to resemble me, and I ascended the Tour Eiffel in an elevator. I consumed hors d'œuvres at the Brasserie Universelle. I attended a band concert in the Tuileries Gardens. I dined with Olive Fremstad at the Mercedes and Olive Fremstad dined with me at the Café d'Harcourt. I heard Salome at the Châtelet, Richard Strauss conducting, with Emmy Destinn as the protagonist in a modest costume, trimmed with fur, which had been designed, it was announced, by the Emperor of Germany. I discovered the Restaurant Cou-Cou, which I have described in The Merry-Go-Round, and I made pilgrimages to the Rat Mort, the Nouvelle Athènes, and the Elysée Montmartre, sacred to the memory of George Moore. They appeared to have altered since he confessed as a young man. I stood on a table at the Bal Tabarin and watched the quadrille, the pas de quatre, concluding with the grand écart, which was once sinister and wicked but which has come, through the portentous solemnity with which tradition has invested it, to have almost a religious significance. I learned to drink Amer Picon, grenadine, and white absinthe. I waited three hours in the street before Liane de Pougy's hotel in the Rue de la Néva to see that famous beauty emerge to take her drive, and I waited nearly as long at the stage-door of the Opéra-Comique for a glimpse of the exquisite Régina Badet. I embarked on one of the joyous little Seine boats and I went slumming in the Place d'Italie, La Villette, a suburb associated in the memory with the name of Yvette Guilbert and Belleville. I saw that very funny farce, Vous n'avez rien à declarer at the Nouveautés. In the Place des Vosges, I admired the old brick houses, among the few that Napoleon and the Baron Haussmann spared in their deracination of Paris. On days when I felt poor, I dined with the cochers at some marchand de vins. On days when I felt rich, I dined with the cocottes at the Café de Paris. I examined the collection of impressionist paintings at the house of Monsieur Durand-Ruel, No. 37, Rue de Rome, and the vast accumulation of unfinished sketches for a museum of teratology at the house of Gustave Moreau, No. 14, Rue de La Rochefoucauld, room after room of unicorns, Messalinas, muses, magi, Salomes, sphinxes, argonauts, centaurs, mystic flowers, chimerae, Semeles, hydras, Magdalens, griffins, Circes, ticpolongas, and crusaders. I drank tea in the Ceylonese tea-room in the Rue Caumartin, where coffee-hued Orientals with combs in their hair waited on the tables. I gazed longingly into the show-windows of the shops where Toledo cigarette-oases, Bohemian garnets, and Venetian glass goblets were offered for sale. I bought a pair of blue velvet workman's trousers, a béret, and a pair of canvas shoes at Au Pays, 162 Faubourg St. Martin. I often enjoyed my chocolate and omelet at the Café de la Régence, where everybody plays chess or checkers and has played chess or checkers for a century or two, and where the actors of the Comédie Française, which is just across the Place, frequently, during a rehearsal, come in their makeup for lunch. I learned the meaning of flic, gigolette, maquereau, tapette, and rigolo. I purchased a dirty silk scarf and a pair of Louis XV brass candlesticks, which I still possess, in the Marché du Temple. I tasted babas au rhum, napoléons, and palmiers. I ordered a suit, which I never wore, from a French tailor for 150 francs. I bought some Brittany ware in an old shop back of Notre-Dame. I admired the fifteenth century apocalyptic glass in the Sainte-Chapelle and the thirteenth century glass in the Cathedral at Chartres. I learned that demi-tasse is an American word, that Sparkling Burgundy is an American drink, and that I did not like French beer. I stayed away from the receptions at the American embassy. I was devout in Saint Sulpice, the Russian Church in the Rue Daru, Saint Germain-des-Prés, Saint Eustache, Sacré-Cœur, and Saint Jacques, and I attended a wedding at the Madeleine, which reminded me that Bel Ami had been married there. I passed pleasant evenings at the Boîte à Fursy, on the Rue Pigalle, and Les Noctambules, on the Rue Champollion. I learned to speak easily of Mayol, Eve Lavallière, Dranem, Ernest la Jeunesse, Colette Willy, Max Dearly, Charles-Henry Hirsch, Lantelme, André Gide, and Jeanne Bloch. I saw Clemenceau, Edward VII, and the King of Greece. I nibbled toasted scones at a tea-shop on the Rue de Rivoli. I met the Steins. In short, you will observe that I did everything that young Americans do when they go to Paris.

On a certain afternoon, early in June, I found myself sitting at a table in the Café de la Paix with Englewood Jennings and Frederic Richards two of my new friends. Richards is a famous person today and even then he was somebody. He had a habit of sketching, wherever he might be, on a sheet of paper at a desk at the Hotel Continental or on a program at the theatre. He drew quick and telling likenesses in a few lines of figures or objects that pleased him, absent-mindedly signed them, and then tossed them aside. This habit of his was so well-known that he was almost invariably followed by admirers of his work, who snapped up his sketches as soon as he had disappeared. I saw a good collection of them, drawn on the stationery of hotels from Hamburg to Taormina, and even on meat paper, go at auction in London a year or so ago for £1,000. When I knew him, Richards was a blond giant, careless of everything except his appearance. Jennings was an American socialist from Harvard who was ranging Europe to interview Jean Jaurès, Gioyanni Papini, and Karl Liebknecht. He was exceedingly eccentric in his dress, had steel-grey eyes, the longest, sharpest nose I have ever seen, and wore glasses framed in tortoise-shell.

It had become my custom to pass two hours of every afternoon on this busy corner, first ordering tea with two brioches, and later a succession of absinthes, which I drank with sugar and water. In time I learned to do without the sugar, just as eventually I might have learned, in all probability, to do without the water, had I not been compelled to do without the absinthe.[1] I was enjoying my third pernod while my companions were dallying with whisky and soda. We were gossiping, and where in the world can one gossip to better advantage than on this busy corner, where every passerby offers a new opportunity? But, occasionally, the conversation slipped into alien channels.

How can the artist, Jennings, for instance, was asking, know that he is inspired, when neither the public nor the critics recognize inspiration? The question is equally interesting asked backwards. As a matter of fact, the artist is sometimes conscious that he is doing one thing, while he is acclaimed and appreciated for doing another. Columbus did not set out to discover America. Yes, there is often an accidental quality in great art and oftener still there is an accidental appreciation of it. In one sense art is curiously bound up with its own epoch, but appreciation or depreciation of its relation to that epoch may come in another generation. The judgment of posterity may be cruel to contemporary genius. In a few years we may decide that Richard Strauss is only another Liszt and Stravinsky, another Rubinstein.

---

1. Since absinthe has come under the ban in Paris, I am informed that the correct form of approach is to ask not for a pernod, but for un distingué.

Inspiration! Richards shrugged his broad shepherd's plaid shoulders. Inspiration! Artists, critics, public, clever men, and philistines monotonously employ that word, but it seems to me that art is created through memory out of experience, combined with a capacity for feeling and expressing experience, and depending on the artist's physical condition at the time when he is at work.

Are you, I asked, one of those who believes that a novelist must be unfaithful to his wife before he can write a fine novel, that a girl should have an amour with a prize-fighter before she can play Juliet, and that a musician must be a pederast before he can construct a great symphony?

Richards laughed.

No, he replied, I am not, but that theory is very popular. How many times I have heard it thundered forth! As a matter of fact, there is a certain amount of truth in it, the germ, indeed, of a great truth, for some emotional experience is essential to the artist, but why particularize? Each as he may!

I know a man, I went on, who doesn't believe that experience has anything to do with art at all. He thinks art is a matter of arrangement and order and form.

His art then, broke in Jennings, is epistemological rather than inspirational.

But what does he arrange? queried Richards. Surely incidents and emotions.

Not at all. He arranges objects, abstractions: colours and reaping-machines, perfumes and toys.

Long ago I read a book like that, Jennings went on. It was called Imperial Purple and it purported to be a history of the Roman Empire or the Roman Emperors. It was a strangely amusing book, rather like a clot of blood on a daisy or a faded pomegranate flower in a glass of buttermilk.

At this period, I avidly collected labels. Who wrote it? I asked.

I don't remember, but your description of your friend recalls the book. What is the name of your friend's book?

He hasn't written a book yet.

I see.

He is about to write it. He knows what he wants to do and he is collecting the materials. He is arranging the form.

What's it about? Jennings appeared to be interested.

Oh, it's about things. Whiffle told me, I suppose he was joking, that it would be about three hundred pages.

Richards set down his glass and in his face I recognized the portentous expression of a man about to be delivered of an epigram. It came: I dislike pineapples, women with steatopygous figures, and men with a gift for paronomasia.

Jennings ignored this ignoble interruption. George Moore has written somewhere, he said, that if an author talks about *what* he is going to write, usually he writes it, but when he talks about *how* he is going to write it, that is the end of the matter. I wonder if this is true? I have never thought much about it before but I think perhaps it is. I think your friend will never write his book.

Richards interrupted again: Look at that maquereau. That's the celebrated French actor who went to America after a brilliant career in France in the more lucrative of his two professions, which ended in a woman's suicide. His history was well-known to the leading woman of the company with which he was to play in America, but she had never met him. At the first rehearsal, when they were introduced, she remarked, Monsieur, la connaissance est déjà faite! Turning aside, he boasted to his male companions, La gueuse! Avant dix jours je l'aurai enfilée! In a week he had made good his threat and in two weeks the poor woman was without a pearl.

He should meet Arabella Munson, said Jennings. She is always willing to pay her way. She fell in love with an Italian sculptor, or at any rate selected him as a suitable father for a prospective child. When she became pregnant, the young man actually fell ill with fear at the thought that he might be compelled to support both Arabella and the baby. He took to his bed and sent his mother as an ambassadress for Arabella's mercy. Choking with sobs, the old woman demanded what would be required of her son. My good woman, replied Arabella, dry your tears. I make it a point of honour never to take a penny from the fathers of my children. Not only do I support the children, often I support their fathers as well!

It was sufficiently warm. I lazily sipped my absinthe. The terrasse was crowded and there was constant movement; as soon as a table was relinquished, another group sat down in the empty chairs. Ephra Vogelsang, a pretty American singer, had just arrived with a pale young blond boy, whom I identified as Marcel Moszkowski, the son of the Polish composer. Presently, another table was taken by Vance Thompson and Ernest la Jeunesse, whose fat face was sprinkled with pimples and whose fat fingers were encased to the knuckles in heavy oriental rings. I bowed to Ephra and to Vance Thompson. On the sidewalk marched the eternal procession of newsboys, calling La Pa—trie! La Pa—trie! so like a phrase at the beginning of the second act of Carmen, old gentlemen, nursemaids, painted boys, bankers, Americans, Germans, Italians, South Americans, Roumanians, and Neo-Kaffirs. The carriages, the motors, the buses, formed a perfect maze on the boulevard. In one of the vehicles I caught a glimpse of another acquaintance.

That's Lily Hampton, I noted. She is the only woman who ever made Toscanini smile. You must understand, to appreciate the story, that she is highly respectable, the Mrs. Kendal of the opera stage, and the mother of eight or nine children. She never was good at languages, speaks them all with a rotten accent and a complete ignorance of their idioms. On this occasion, she was singing in Italian but she was unable to converse with the director in his native tongue and, consequently, he was giving her directions in French. He could not, however, make her understand what he wanted her to do. Again and again he repeated his request. At last she seemed to gather his meaning, that she was to turn her back to the footlights. What she asked him, however, ran like this: Est-ce que vous voulez mon derrière, maestro?

Now there was a diversion, an altercation at the further end of the terrasse, and a fluttering of feathered, flowered, and smooth-haired and bald heads turned in that direction. In the midst of this turbulence, I heard my name being called and, looking up, beheld Peter Whiffle waving from the impériale of a bus. I beckoned him to descend and join us and this he contrived to do after the bus had travelled several hundred yards on its way towards the Madeleine and I had abandoned the idea of seeing him return. But the interval gave me time to inform Richards and Jennings that this was the young author of whom I had spoken. Presently he came along, strolling languidly down the walk. He looked a bit tired, but he was very smartly dressed, with a gardenia as a boutonnière, and he seemed to vibrate with a feverish kind of jauntiness.

I *am* glad to see you, he cried. I've been meaning to look you up. In fact if I hadn't met you I should have looked you up tonight. I'm burning for adventures. What are you doing?

I explained that I was doing nothing at all and introduced him to my friends. Jennings had an engagement. He explained that he had to talk

CARL VAN VECHTEN

at some socialist meeting, called our waiter, paid for his pile of saucers, and took his departure. Richards confessed that he was burning too.

What shall we do? asked the artist.

There's plenty to do, announced Peter, confidently; almost too much for one night. But let's hurry over to Serapi's, before he closes his shop.

We asked no questions. We paid our saucers, rose, and strolled along with Peter across the Place in front of the Opéra and down the Rue de la Chaussée-d'Antin until we stood before a tiny shop, the window of which was filled with bottles of perfume and photographs of actresses and other great ladies of various worlds and countries, all inscribed with flamboyant encomiums, relating to the superior merits of Serapi's wares and testifying to the superlative esteem in which Serapi himself was held.

Led by Peter, in the highest exuberance of nervous excitement but still, I thought, looking curiously tired, we passed within the portal. We found ourselves in a long narrow room, surrounded on two sides by glass cases, in which, on glass shelves, were arranged the products of the perfumer's art. At the back, there was a cashier's desk without an attendant; at the front, the show-window. In the centre of the room, the focus of a group of admiring women, stood a tawny-skinned Oriental—perhaps concretely an Arabian—with straight black hair and soft black eyes. His physique was magnificent and he wore a morning coat. Obviously, this was Serapi himself.

Peter, who had now arrived at a state in which he could with difficulty contain his highly wrought emotion—and it was at this very moment that I began to suspect him of collecting amusements along with his other objects—, in a whisper confirmed my conjecture. The ladies, delicately fashioned Tanagra statuettes in tulle and taffeta and chiffon artifices from the smartest shops, in hats on which bloomed all the posies of the season and posies which went beyond any which had ever bloomed, were much too attractive to be duchesses, although right here I must pause to protest that even duchesses sometimes have their good points: the Duchess of Talleyrand has an ankle and the Duchess of Marlborough, a throat. The picture, to be recalled later when Mina Loy gave me her lovely drawing of Eros being spoiled by women, was so pleasant, withal slightly ridiculous, that Richards and I soon caught the infection of Peter's scarcely masked laughter and our eyes, too, danced. We made some small pretence of examining the jars and bottles of Scheherazade, Ambre, and Chypre in the cases, but only a small pretence was necessary, as the ladies and their Arab paid not the slightest attention to us.

At length, following a brief apology, Serapi broke through the ranks and disappeared through a doorway behind the desk at the back of the room. As the curtains lifted, I caught a glimpse of a plain, business-like woman, too dignified to be a mere clerk, obviously the essential wife of the man of genius. He was gone only a few seconds but during those seconds the chatter ceased abruptly. It was apparent that the ladies had come singly. They were not acquainted with one another. As Serapi reentered, they chirped again, peeped and twittered their twiddling tune, the words of which were Ah! and Oh! In one hand, he carried a small crystal phial to which a blower was attached. He explained that the perfume was his latest creation, an hermetic confusion of the dangers and ardours of Eastern life and death, the concentrated essence of the unperfumed flowers of Africa, the odour of their colours, he elaborated, wild desert existence, the mouldering tombs of the kings of Egypt, the decaying laces of a dozen Byzantine odalisques, a fragrant breath or two from the hanging gardens of Babylon, and a faint suggestion of the perspiration of Istar. It is my reconstruction, the artist concluded, of the perfume which Ruth employed to attract Boaz! The recipe is an invention based on a few half-illegible lines which I discovered in the beauty-table book of an ancient queen of Georgia, perhaps that very Thamar whose portrait has been painted in seductive music by the Slav composer, Balakireff.

The ladies gasped. The fascinating Arab pressed the rubber bulb and blew the cloying vapours into their faces, adjuring them, at the same time, to think of Thebes or Haroun-Al-Raschid or the pre-Adamite sultans. The room was soon redolent with a heavy vicious odour which seemed to reach the brain through the olfactory nerves and to affect the will like ether.

He is the only man alive today, whispered Peter, not without reverence, who has taken Flaubert's phrase seriously. He passes his nights dreaming of larger flowers and stranger perfumes. I believe that he could invent a new vice!

Serapi went the round of the circle with his mystic spray, and the twitterings of the ladies softened to ecstatic coos, like the little coos of dismay and delight of female cats who feel the call of pleasure; when suddenly the phial fell from the Arab's unclasped hand, the hand itself dropped to his side, the brown skin became a vivid green, all tension left his body, and he crumbled into a heap on the floor. The ladies shrieked; there was a delicious, susurrous, rainbow swirl and billow of tulle and taffeta and chiffon; there was a frantic nodding and waving of sweet-peas, red roses, dandelions, and magenta bell-flowers; and eight pairs of white-gloved arms circled rhythmically in the air. The effect was worthy of the Russian Ballet and, had Fokine been present, it would doubtless have been perpetuated to the subsequent enjoyment of audiences at Covent Garden and the Paris Opéra.

Now, an assured and measured step was heard. From a room in the rear, the calm, practical presence entered, bearing a glass of water. The ladies moved a little to one side as she knelt before the recumbent figure and sprinkled the green face. Serapi almost immediately began to manifest signs of recovery; his muscles began to contract and his face regained its natural colour. We made our way into the open air and the warm western sunlight of the late afternoon. Peter was choking with laughter. I was chuckling. Richards was too astonished to express himself.

Life is sometimes artistic, Peter was saying. Sometimes, if you give it a chance and look for them, it makes patterns, beautiful patterns. But Serapi excelled himself today. He has never done anything like this before. I shall never go back there again. It would be an anticlimax.

We dined somewhere, where I have forgotten. It is practically the only detail of that evening which has escaped my memory. I remember clearly how Richards sat listening in silent amazement to Peter's arguments and decisions on dreams and circumstances, erected on bewilderingly slender hypotheses. He built up, one after another, the most gorgeous and fantastic temples of theory; five minutes later he demolished them with a sledge-hammer or a feather. It was gay talk, fancy wafted from nowhere, unimportant, and vastly entertaining. Indeed, who has ever talked like Peter?

We seemed to be in his hands. At any rate neither Richards nor I offered any suggestions. We waited to hear him tell us what we were to do. About 9 o'clock, while we were sipping our cognac, he informed us that our next destination would be La Cigale, a music hall on the outer circle of the boulevards in Montmartre, where there was to be seen a revue called, Nue Cocotte, of which I still preserve the poster, drawn by Maës Laïa, depicting a fat duenna, fully dressed, wearing a red wig and adorned with pearls, and carrying a lorgnette, a more plausible female, nude, but for a hat, veil, feather boa, and a pair of high boots with yellow tops over which protrude an inch or two of blue sock, and an English comic, in a round hat, a yellow checked suit, bearing binoculars, all three astride a remarkably vivid red hobby horse whose feet are planted in the attitude of bucking. The comic grasps the bobbed black tail of the nag in one hand and the long yellow braid of the female in the other.

The cocottes of the period were wont to wear very large bell-shaped hats. Lily Elsie, who was appearing in The Merry Widow in London, followed this fashion and, as a natural consequence, these head-decorations were soon dubbed, probably by an American, Merry Widow hats. Each succeeding day, some girl would appear on the boulevards surmounted by a greater monstrosity than had been seen before. Discussion in regard to the subject, editorial and epistolary, raged at the moment in the Paris journals.

Once we were seated in our stalls on the night in question, it became evident that the hat of the cocotte in front of Peter completely obscured his view of the stage. He bent forward and politely requested her to remove it. She turned and explained with equal politeness and a most entrancing smile that she could not remove her hat without removing her hair, surely an impossibility, Monsieur would understand. Monsieur understood perfectly but, under the circumstances, would Madame have any objection if Monsieur created a disturbance? Madame, her eyes shining with mirth, replied that she would not have the tiniest objection, that above all else in life she adored fracases. They were of a delight to her. At this juncture in the interchange of compliments the curtain rose disclosing a row of females in mauve dresses, bearing baskets of pink roses. Presently the compère appeared.

Chapeau! cried, Peter, in the most stentorian voice I have ever heard him assume. Chapeau!

The spectators turned to look at the valiant American. Several heads nodded sympathy and approval.

Chapeau! Peter called again, pointing to the adorable little lady in front of him, who was enjoying the attention she had created. Her escort, on the other hand, squirmed a little.

The cry was now taken up by other unfortunate gentlemen in the stalls, who were placed in like situations but who had not had the courage to begin the battle. The din, indeed, soon gained such a degree of dynamic force that not one word of what was being said on the stage, not one note of the music, could be distinguished. Gesticulating figures stood up in every part of the theatre, shrieking and frantically waving canes. The compère advanced to the footlights and appeared to be addressing us, much in the manner of an actor attempting to stem a fire stampede in a playhouse, but, of course, he was inaudible. As he stepped back, a sudden lull succeeded to the tumult. Peter took advantage of this happy quiet to interject: Comme Mélisande, je ne suis pas heureux ici!

The spectators roared and screamed; the house rocked with their mirth. Even the mimes were amused. Now, escorted by two of his secretaries in elaborate coats decorated with much gold braid, the manager of the theatre appeared, paraded solemnly down the aisle to our seats and, with a bow, offered us a box, which we accepted at once and in which we received homage for the remainder of the evening. At last we could see the stage and enjoy the blond Idette Bremonval, the brunette Jane Merville, the comic pranks of Vilbert and Prince, and the Festival of the Déesse Raison.

The performance concluded, the pretty lady who had not removed her hat, commissioned her reluctant escort to inquire if we would not step out for a drink with them. The escort was not ungracious but, obviously, he lacked enthusiasm. The lady, just as obviously, had taken a great fancy to Peter. We went to the Rat Mort, where we sat on the terrasse, the lady gazing steadily at her new hero and laughing immoderately at his every sally. Peter, however, quickly showed that he was restless and presently he rose, eager to seek new diversions. We hailed a passing fiacre and jumped in, while the lady waved us pathetic adieux. Her companion seemed distinctly relieved by our departure. Peter was now in the highest animal spirits. All traces of fatigue had fled from his face. The horse which drew our fiacre was a poor, worn-out brute, like so many others in Paris, and the cocher, unlike so many others in Paris, was kind-hearted and made no effort to hasten his pace. We were crawling down the hill.

I will race you! cried Peter, leaping out (he told me afterwards that he had once undertaken a similar exploit with a Bavarian railway train).

Meet me at the Olympia Bar! he cried, dashing on ahead.

The cocher grunted, shook his head, mumbled a few unintelligible words to the horse, and we drove on more slowly than before. Peter, indeed, was soon out of sight.

Ten minutes later, as we entered the café under the Olympia Music Hall, we noted with some surprise that the stools in front of the bar, on which the cocottes usually sat with their feet on the rungs, their trains dragging the floor, were empty. The crowd had gathered at the other end of the long hall and the centre of the crowd was Peter. He was holding a reception, a reception of cocottes!

Ah! Good evening, Mademoiselle Rolandine de Maupreaux, he was saying as he extended his hand, I am delighted to greet you here tonight. And if this isn't dear little Mademoiselle Célestine Sainte-Résistance and her charming friend, Mademoiselle Edmée Donnez-Moi! And Camille! Camille la Grande! Quelle chance de vous voir! Et Madame, votre mère, elle va bien? Et Gisèle la Belle! Mais vous avez oublié de m'écrire! Do not, I pray you, neglect me again. And the charming Hortense des Halles et de chez Maxim, and the particularly adorable Abélardine de Belleville et de la Place d'Italie. Votre sœur va mieux, j'espére. Then, drawing us in, permettezmoi, mesdemoiselles, de vous presenter mes amis, le Duc de Rochester et le Comte de Cedar Rapids. Spécialement, mesdemoiselles, permettez-moi de vous recommander le Comte de Cedar Rapids.

He had never, of course, seen any of them before, but they liked it.

Richards grumbled, It's bloody silly, but he was laughing harder than I was.

I heard one of the girls say, Le jeune Américain est fou!

And the antiphony followed, Mais il est charmant.

Later, another remarked, Je crois que je vais lui demander de me faire une politesse!

Overhearing which, Peter rejoined, Avec plaisir, Mademoiselle. Quel genre?

It was all gay, irresponsible and meaningless, perhaps, but *gay*. We sat at tables and drank and smoked and spun more fantasies and quaint conceits until a late hour, and that night I learned that even French cocottes will occasionally waste their time, provided they are sufficiently diverted. Towards four o'clock in the morning, however, I began to note a change in Peter's deportment and demeanour. There were moments when he sat silent, a little aloof, seemingly the prey of a melancholy regret, too well aware, perhaps, that the atmosphere he had himself created would suck him into its merry hurricane. I caught the lengthening shadows under his eyes and the premonitory hollows in his cheeks. And this time, therefore, it was I who suggested departure. Peter acceded, but with an air of wistfulness as if even the effort of moving from an uncomfortable situation were painful to him. Rising, we kissed our hands to the band of sirens, who all pressed forward like the flower maidens of Parsifal and with equal success. Three of the pretty ladies accompanied us upstairs to the sidewalk and every one of the three kissed Peter on the mouth, but not one of them offered to kiss Richards or me.

We engaged another fiacre and drove up the Champs-Elysées. Now, it was Richards and I who had become vibrant. Peter was silent and old and apart. The dawn, the beautiful indigo dawn of Paris was upon us. The cool trees were our only companions in the deserted streets until, near the great grey arch, we began to encounter the wagons laden with vegetables, bound for the Halles, wagons on which carrots, parsnips, turnips, onions, radishes and heads of lettuce were stacked in orderly and intricate patterns. The horses, the reins drooping loosely over their backs, familiar with the route, marched slowly down the wide avenue, while the drivers in their blue smocks, perched high on the fronts of their carts, slept. We drove past them up the Avenue du Bois-de-Boulogne into the broadening daylight. On Peter Whiffle's countenance were painted the harsh grey lines of misery and despair.

V

Notwithstanding that Peter occupied an undue share of my waking thoughts for the next few days, perhaps a week went by before I found it convenient to seek him out again. One afternoon, I shook myself free from other entertainments and made my way in a taxi-auto to the apartment in the street near the Rue Blanche. The concierge, who was knitting at a little window adjacent to the door, informed me that to the best of her belief Monsieur Whiffle was at home. Venturing to operate the ascenseur alone, I was somewhat proud of my success in reaching the fourth floor without accident. Standing before Peter's door, I could hear the sound of a woman's voice, singing Manon's farewell to her little table:

> *Adieu, notre petite table,*
> *Qui nous réunit si souvent!*
> *Adieu, notre petite table,*
> *Si grande pour nous cependant.*
> *On tient, c'est inimaginable,*
> *Si peu de place en se serrant.*

The voice was a somewhat uncertain soprano with a too persistent larmoyante quality. When it ceased, I pressed the button and the door was opened by Peter, in violet and grey striped pyjamas and Japanese straw sandals with purple velvet straps across his toes.

Van Vechten! he cried. It's you! We've been home all day. Clara's been singing.

So the voice was Clara's. She sat, indeed, on the long piano bench—the piano was an acquisition since my last visit—, also slightly clad. She was wearing, to be exact, a crêpe de chine night-dress. Her feet were bare and her hair was loose but, as the day was cool, she had thrown across her shoulders a black Manila shawl, embroidered with huge flowers of Chinese vermilion and magenta.

How are you, Mr. Van Vechten? she asked, extending her hand. I'll get some tea. Her manner, I noted, was more ingratiating than it had been the day we met at Martha's.

Nothing whatever was said about the situation, if there was a situation. For my part, I may say that I was entirely unaccustomed to walking into an apartment at five o'clock in the afternoon and discovering the host in pyjamas, conversing intimately with a lightly-clad lady, who, a week earlier, I had every reason to believe, had been only a casual acquaintance. The room, too, had been altered. The piano, a Pleyel baby grand, occupied a space near the window and George Moore was sitting on it, finding it an excellent point of vantage from which to scan the happenings in the outside world. Naturally his back was turned and he did not get up, taking his air of indifference from Peter and Clara or, perhaps, they had taken their air from him. The note-books had disappeared, although a pile of miscellaneous volumes, on top of which I spied Jean Lombard's l'Agonie, still occupied the corner. The table was covered with a cloth and the remains of a lunch, which had evidently consisted of veal kidneys, toast, and coffee. I detected the odour of Cœur de Jeannette and presently I descried a brûle-parfum, a tiny jade dragon, valiantly functioning. A pair of long white suède gloves and a black hat with a grey feather decorated the clock and candelabra on the mantelshelf, and a black and white check skirt, a pair of black silk stockings, and low patent-leather lady's shoes in trees were also to be seen, lying over a chair and on the floor.

Peter, however, attempted no explanations. Indeed, none was required, except perhaps for a catechumen. He began to talk immediately, in an easy conversational tone, evidently trying to cover my confusion. His manner reminded me that an intelligent Negro, who had written many books and met many people, had once told me that he was always obliged to spend at least ten minutes putting new white acquaintances at their ease, making them feel that it was unnecessary for them to put him at his ease. It is a curious fact that the man in an embarrassing situation is seldom as embarrassed as the man who breaks in upon it.

Peter asked many questions about what I had been doing, inquired about Richards, whom he avowed he liked—they had not, I afterwards recalled, exchanged more than three words—, and concluded with a sort of rhapsody on Clara's voice, which he pronounced magnificently suited to the new music.

Presently Clara herself came back into the room, bearing a tray with a pot of tea, toast and petits fours. She placed her burden on the piano bench while she quickly swept the débris from the table. Then she transferred the tea service to the unoccupied space and we drew up our chairs.

Where have you been? asked Clara. Martha says she hasn't seen you. Will you have one lump or two?

Two. You know, when one comes to Paris for the first time—

I took Van Vechten about a bit the other night, Peter broke in. I think I forgot to tell you. We've had so much to talk about. . .

Clara interrupted the shadow of an anserine smile to nibble a pink cake. Her legs protruded at an odd angle and I caught myself looking at her thick ankles.

You're looking at my legs! she exclaimed. You mustn't do that! I have very ugly legs.

But they're very sympathetic! cried Peter. Don't you think they're sympathetic, Van Vechten?

I assured him that I did and we went on talking, a little constrainedly, I thought, about nothing in particular, until, at length, Peter asked Clara if she would sing again. Without waiting for a reply, he seated himself before the piano and began the prelude to Manon's air in the Cours la Reine scene and Clara, without rising, sang:

Je marche sur tous les chemins
Aussi bien qu'une souveraine;
On s'incline, on baise mes mains,
Car par la beauté je suis reine!

Now her voice had lost the larmoyante quality, which evidently was a part of her bag of tricks for more emotional song, but it had acquired a hard brilliancy which was even more disagreeable to the ear. She had also, I remarked, no great regard for the pitch and little, if any, expressiveness. Nevertheless, Peter wheeled around, after an accompaniment which was even less sympathetic to me than Clara's legs, to exclaim:

Superb! I want her to study Isolde.

Peter doesn't understand, explained Clara, that you must begin with the lighter parts. If I sang Isolde now I would have no voice in five years. Isolde will come later. I can sing Isolde after I have lost my voice. My first rôles will be Manon, Violetta, and Juliette. It's old stuff, perhaps, but it doesn't injure the voice, and the voice is my first consideration. Now I wouldn't sing Salome if they offered me 500 francs a night.

Did you hear about Adelina Patti? asked Peter. She is a good Catholic. She went to a performance of Salome at the Châtelet and while Destinn was osculating the head of Jochanaan she dropped to her knees in her loge and began to pray!

I don't blame her, said Clara. It's rotten and immoral, Salome—not the play, I don't mean that, but the music, rotten, immoral music, ruinous to the voice. Patti was probably praying God for another Rossini. Strauss's music will steal ten years from Destinn's career.

Peter eyed her with adoration. After a few more remarks, I made my departure, both of them urging me to come again at any time. Peter had not said one word about his writing, I reflected, as I walked down the stairs, and he had been very exaggerated in his praise of Clara's meagre talents.

And I did not go back. I did not see Peter again that summer; I did not see him again, in fact, for nearly six years. My further adventures, which included a trip to London, to Munich, where I attended the Wagner and Mozart festivals, to Holland and Belgium, were sufficiently diverting but, as they have no bearing on Peter's history, I shall not relate them now. They will fall into their proper chapters in my autobiography, which Alfred A. Knopf will publish in two volumes in the fall of 1936.

Although I did not learn the facts I am about to catalogue until a much later date—some of them, indeed, not until after Peter's death—this seems as good a place as any to tell what I know of his early life. He was born June 5, 1885, in Toledo, Ohio. He never told his age to any one and I only discovered it after his death. If an inquiry were made concerning it, it was his custom to counter with another question: How old do you think I am? and then to add one year to the reply, thus insuring credence. So I have heard him give himself ages varying from eighteen to forty-five, but he was only thirty-four when he died in 1919.

His father was cashier in a bank, a straight, serious, plain sort of man, of the kind that is a prop to a small town, looked up to and respected, asked whether an election will have an effect on stock values, and whether it is better to illuminate one's house with gas or electricity. His mother was a small woman with a pleasant face and red hair which she parted in the centre. Kindliness she occasionally carried almost to the point of silliness. She was somewhat garrulous, too, but she was well-read, not at all ignorant, and at surprising moments gave evidence of possessing a small stock of common sense. I think Peter inherited a good deal of his quality from his mother, who was a Fotheringay of West Chester, Pennsylvania. I met her for the first time soon after her husband's death. She was wearing, in addition to a suitable mourning garment, five chains of Chinese beads and seemed moderately depressed.

Peter's resemblance to Buridan's donkey (it will be remembered that the poor beast wavered between the hay and the water until he starved to death) began with his very birth. He could not, indeed, decide whether he would be born or not. The family physician, by the aid of science and the knife, decided the matter for him. Soon thereafter he often hesitated between the milk-bottle and the breast. There was, doubtless, a certain element of restlessness and curiosity connected with this vacillation, a desire to miss nothing in life. It is possible that the root of this aggressive instinct might have been deracinated but Mrs. Whiffle, with a foresense of the decrees of the most modern motherhood, held no brief for suppressed desires. Baby Peter was always permitted to choose, at least nearly always, and so, as he grew older, his mania developed accordingly. A decision actually caused him physical pain, often made him definitely ill. He would pause interminably before two toys in a shop, or at any rate until his mother bought both of them for him. He could never decide whether to go in or go out, whether to play horse or to cut out pictures. His mother has told me that on one occasion she discovered this precocious child (at the age of twelve) in the library of a Toledo bibliophile (she was in the house as a luncheon guest) with the Sonnets of Pietro Aretino in one hand and Fanny Hill in the other. He could not make up his mind from which he would derive the most pleasure. In this instance, his maternal parent intervened and took both books away from him.

Otherwise, aside from various slight illnesses, his childhood was singularly devoid of incident. Because he hummed bits of tune while at play, his mother decided that he must be musical and sent him to an instructor of the piano. The first six months were drudgery for Peter but as soon as he began to read music easily the skies cleared for him. He never became a great player but he played easily and well, much better than I imagined after hearing his rather bombastic accompaniments to Clara's singing. Of books he was an omnivorous reader. He read every volume—some of them two or three times—in the family library, which included, of course, the works of Dickens, Thackeray, Wilkie Collins, Charles Reade, and Sir Walter Scott, Emerson's Essays, Bulwer-Lytton, Owen Meredith's Lucile, that long narrative poem called Nothing to Wear, Artemus Ward's Panorama, Washington Irving, Longfellow, Whittier, Thoreau, Lowell, and Hawthorne, and among the moderns, Mark Twain, William Dean Howells, F. Hopkinson Smith, F. Marion Crawford, Richard Harding Davis, George W. Cable, Frank Stockton, H. C. Bunner, and Thomas Nelson Page. Peter once told me that his favourite books when he was fourteen or fifteen years old were Sarah Grand's The Heavenly Twins and H. B. Fuller's The Chevalier of Pensieri-Vani. The latter made a remarkable impression on him, when he first discovered it at the age of fifteen, not that he fully appreciated its ironic raillery but it seemed to point out the pleasure to be apprehended from pleasant places. He named a cat of the period, a regal yellow short-haired tom, after the Prorege of Arcopia. The house library exhausted, the public library offered further opportunities for browsing and it was there that he made the acquaintance of Gautier, in translation, of course. He also found it possible to procure—though not at the public library—and he devoured with avidity—he has asserted that they had an extraordinary effect in awakening his imagination— Nick Carter, Bertha M. Clay, and Golden Days. For a period of four or five years, in spite of all protests, although he had never heard of the vegetarians, he subsisted entirely on a diet of cookies soaked in hot milk. He had a curious inherent dislike for spinach and it was characteristic of his father that he ordered the dish to appear on the table every day until the boy tasted a morsel. In after life, Peter could never even look at a dish of spinach. He cared nothing at all for outdoor sports. Games of any kind, card or osculatory, he considered nuisances. At a party, while the other children were engaged in the pleasing pastime of post office, he was usually to be found in a corner, reading some book. The companionship of boys and girls of his own age meant very little to him. He liked to talk to older people and found special pleasure in the company of the Reverend Horatio Wallace, a clergyman of the Dutch Reformed Church, who had visited New York. This reverend doctor was violently opposed to art museums, novels, and symphony orchestras, but he talked about them and he was the only person Peter knew in Toledo who did. He railed against the sins of New York and the vices of Paris but, also, he described them.

In the matter of a university education, his mother took a high hand, precluding all discussion and indecision by sending him willy-nilly to Williams. Her brother had been a Williams man and she prayed that Peter might like to be one too. The experiment was not unsuccessful. The charm in Peter's nature began to expand at college and he even made a few friends, the names of most of which he could no longer remember, when he spoke to me of his college days some years afterwards. He realized that the reason he had made so few in Toledo was that the people of Toledo were not his kind of people. They lived in a world which did not exist for him. They lived in the world of Toledo while he lived in the world of books. At college, he began to take an interest in personalities; he began to take an interest in life itself. He studied French—it was the only course he thoroughly enjoyed—and he began to read Gautier in the original. Then, at the instigation of a particularly intelligent professor, he passed on to Barbey d'Aurevilly, to Huysmans, to Laforgue, and to Mallarmé.

His holidays were always a torture for the boy. Should he accept one of several invitations to visit his lad friends or should he go home? One Easter vacation, Monkey Rollins had asked him to visit him in Providence while Teddy Quartermouse had bidden him to enjoy himself in New York. Peter pondered. He liked Monkey's sisters but a week in Providence meant, he knew, dancing, bridge, and golf, all of which he hated. Teddy was not as companionable as Monkey and he had no sisters, but in New York both indoor and outdoor sports could be avoided. Peter helplessly examined both sides of the shield until Monkey settled the question by coming after him, helping him pack, and carrying him triumphantly to the railway station.

No sooner, however, had he arrived in Providence than he knew that it would be impossible for him to remain there. He did not find Monkey's mother very agreeable, rather she was too agreeable. The vegetables were cooked in milk—the Rollins family had previously lived in Missouri. This, of course, was not to be borne. Worst of all, there was a parrot, a great, shrieking, feathered beast, with koprolagniac tastes. Nevertheless, he exerted himself at dinner, giving a lengthy and apocryphal description to Mrs. Rollins of his performance of a concerto for kettle-drum with the college band, and doubtless made a distinctly favourable impression on the entire family. Even the parrot volunteered: Hurrah for you, kid, you're some guy! as the procession trooped into the library, which one of the girls referred to as "the carnegie," for coffee. While Caruso negotiated Celeste Aida on the phonograph, Peter, after whispering an appropriate excuse to Monkey, contrived to slip upstairs. He looked about on the landing in the upper hallway for a telephone but, naturally, it wasn't there. Then he reconnoitred and discovered that by climbing out over the porch and making a ten foot jump he would land very neatly in a bed of crocuses. This he did and, scrambling to his feet, made straight for an apothecary's coloured lights, which he saw in the distance. The sequel is simple. In fifteen minutes, by way of the kitchen, he was back in the library; in thirty minutes, he had the family in roars of laughter; in forty-five minutes, Papa Rollins began to yawn and guessed it was bed-time; Mama Rollins called in the maid to cover the parrot and arrange the fire. Monkey said he thought he would play a game of something or other with Peter. The girls giggled. In exactly an hour, there was a ring at the door and the maid reappeared in the library, with a yellow envelope addressed to Peter. He hastily tore it open, trying to look portentous. Everybody else did look portentous. Peter handed the telegram to Monkey, who read it aloud: Your mother would like to shake your hand before she takes the ether tomorrow morning. The message was dated from New York and the signature was that of a famous surgeon. Mrs. Rollins was the first to break a moment of appalling silence: There's a train in fifteen minutes. It's the last. Quick, Monkey, the motor! Peter cried, Send my things to the Manhattan, as he jerked on his coat. He caught the train and some hours later he and Teddy Quartermouse might have been observed amusing themselves with highballs and a couple of girls at Rector's.

In time, college days passed. Peter confessed to me that the last two years were an awful strain but he stuck them out, chiefly because he could not think of anything else he wanted to do. His real mental agony began with his release. He dreaded life and most of all he dreaded work. His father, although well-to-do, had a sharply defined notion that a boy who would not work never amounted to anything. His peculiar nature sometimes asserted itself in ludicrous and fantastically exaggerated demonstrations of this theory. Once, for example, during a summer vacation spent in the country, he insisted that Peter skin a pig. You have an opportunity to learn now and you never can tell when you may have to skin another pig. When the time comes you will be prepared. His father, Peter returned from college discovered, was in no mood to tolerate vacillation or dawdling. But Peter seemed to feel no urge of any kind. I not only did not want to do anything, he explained, there was nothing that I wanted to do. Here his father, with whom the boy had never been particularly sympathetic (motive of the Œdipus complex by the flutes in the orchestra), asserted his authority and put him in the bank. Peter loathed the bank. He hated his work, cutting open envelopes early in the morning, sorting out bills for collection, and then, on his bicycle, making the collections. In the afternoon, an endless task at the adding machine seemed Dantesque and, at night, the sealing of envelopes was even more tiresome than opening them in the morning. There was, however, one mitigating circumstance in connection with the last job of the day, the pleasure afforded by the rich odour of the hot sealing-wax. His pay was $9 a week; he has told me that probably he was not worth it! Fortunately he lived at home and was not asked to pay board. He bought books with the $9 and "silly things." When I asked him what he meant by silly things, he replied: O! Rookwood pottery, and alligators, and tulip bulbs: I don't remember, things like that! One day, he promised his father that he would give up smoking if that one would present him with a gold cigarette-case!

There came a morning when he could not make up his mind to get up. His mother called him several times in vain. He arrived at the bank half an hour late and was reprimanded. His father spoke about his tardiness at lunch. At this period he was inclined to be sulky. He started off on his bicycle in the afternoon but he did not go to the bank. He rode along by the river, stopping at a low saloon in the outlying districts, where the workmen of some factory were wont to congregate in the evening, and drank a great many glasses of beer. Cheered somewhat thereby, the thought of facing his father no longer exasperated him. The big scene took place before dinner. Had it not been for the beer, he would have been obliged to act his part on an empty stomach.

Are you no good at all? Thus his father's baritone aria began. Are you worthless? I'm not going to support you. Suppose you had to pay your own board. I can't keep a son of mine in the bank because he is a son of mine unless he does some work. Certainly not. How long are you going to dawdle? What are you going to do? Et cetera, et cetera, with a magnificent cadenza and a high E to top off with. Sustained by the beer, Peter reported to me that he rather enjoyed the tune. He said nothing. Dinner was eaten in complete silence and then the paternal parent went to bed, a discouraged and broken man. He seemed senescent, although he was not yet fifty. After dinner, Peter's mother spoke to him more gently but she also was full of warning and gloomy foreboding: What is it you want to do, my son? . . . I don't know. I'm not sure that I want to do anything. . . But you must do *something*. You wouldn't be manly if you didn't do something. It is manly to work. A day will come when my son will want to marry and then he will need money to support his dear wife. Etc. Etc. Peter reported to me that he seemed to have heard this music before. He had not yet read The Way of All Flesh; I doubt if it were published at this time, but Ernest Pontifex would have been a sympathetic figure to him. Peter knew the meaning of the word cliché, although the sound and the spelling of it were yet strange to him.

When he got to his room certain words his mother had spoken rang in his ears. Why, he asked himself, should men support women? Art is the only attraction in life and women never do good work in art. They are useless in the world aside from their functions of sex and propagation. Why should they not work so that the males could be free to think and dream? Then it occurred to him that he would be furious if any woman supported his father; that could not be borne, to have his father at home all day while his mother was away at work!

Nevertheless, he went to sleep quite happy, he has assured me, and slept soundly through the night, although he dreamed of a pair of alligators, one of which was pulling at his head and the other at his feet, while a man with an ax rained blows on his stomach. In the morning his affairs seemed to be in a desperate state. He could not bear the idea of getting up and going to the bank and yet there was nothing else he wanted to do. Of one thing only he was sure: he did not want to support himself. He did not, so far as he was able to make out, want to do anything! He wanted his family to stop bothering him. Was no provision made in this world for such as he?

Certainly, no provision was made for him in Toledo, Ohio. The word temperament was still undiscovered there. His negative kind of desire was alien to American sympathy. Of so much, he was aware. Adding machines and collections awaited him. He went to the bank where the paying teller again reprimanded him. So did one of the clerks. So did one of the directors, a friend of his father. He staggered through another day, which he helped along a little by returning at noon with all his notes uncollected. Nobody wants to pay today, he explained. . . But it's your business to make them pay. . . There was cold ham, cold slaw, and rice pudding for lunch. His mother had been crying. His father was stern.

During the rice pudding, he made a resolution, which he kept. From that day on he worked as he had never worked before. Everybody in the bank was astonished. His father was delighted. His mother said, I told you so. I know my son. . . He stopped buying books and silly things and, when he had saved enough money, he took a train to New York without bidding the bank officials or his family good-bye. Once there, his resolution again failed him. He had no desires, or if he had, one counteracted another. His money was almost gone and he was forced to seek for work but everywhere he went he was refused. He lived at a Mills Hotel. He retained a strange fondness for his mother and began to write her, asking her to address him care of general delivery.

At last he secured a position at a soda fountain in a drug-store. He worked there about a week. One night the place got on his nerves to such an extent that he wanted to break the glasses and squirt fizz at every customer. To amuse himself, therefore, he contrived to inject a good dose of castor oil or cantharides into every drink he served. The proprietor of the shop was snoopy, Peter told me, and after watching me out of the corner of his eye for some time, he gave me a good kick, which landed me in the middle of the street. He tossed six dollars, the remainder of my wages, after me. It may appear strange to you but I have never been happier in my life than I was that night with six dollars in my possession and the satisfactory knowledge that I would never see that store again.

During the next three weeks, Peter did not find any work. I doubt if he tried to find any. He often slept in Madison Square or Bryant Park with a couple of newspapers over him and a couple under him. He lived on the most meagre rations, some of which he collected in bread lines. He even begged at the kitchen doors of the large hotels and asked for money on the street. He has told me, however, that he was neither discouraged nor unhappy. He felt the most curious sense of uplift, as if he were suffering martyrdom, as, indeed, he was. Life seemed to have left him out of its accounting, to have made no arrangements for his nature. He had no desire to work, in fact his repugnance for work was his strongest feeling, and yet, it seemed, he could procure no money without working. He was willing, however, to go without the things he wanted, really to suffer, rather than work. I just did not want to do anything, he has said. It was a fixed idea. It was my greatest joy to talk about the social unrest, the rights of the poor, the wicked capitalist, and the ideas of Karl Marx with the man in the street, the real man in the street, the man who never went anywhere else. During this period, he continued to write his mother what she afterwards described as "bright, clever letters." I have seen a few of them, full of the most astounding energy and enthusiasm, and a vague philosophy of quietism. She wrote back, gently chiding him, letters of resignation but still letters of advice, breathing the hope that he might grow into a respected citizen of Toledo, Ohio. She did not understand Peter but she loved him and would have gone to New York to see him, had not a restraining hand burked her. Mr. Whiffle was determined to hold no more traffic with his son. He refused, indeed, to allow Peter's name to be mentioned in his presence. Toledo talked with intensity behind his back but Mr. Whiffle did not know that. Hard as he tried not to show it, he was disappointed: it was impossible for him to reconcile his idea of a son with the actuality. Mrs. Whiffle's first mild suggestion that she might visit Peter was received with a terrible hurricane of resentment. She did not mention the subject again. She would have gone anyway if Peter had asked her to come but he never did.

Through an Italian, whom he met one day in Bryant Park, Peter next secured a position as a member of the claque at the Opera. Every night, with instructions when to applaud, he received either a seat in the dress circle or a general admission ticket. There was also a small salary attached to the office. He did not care about the salary but he enjoyed going to the Opera which he had never before attended. He heard Manon Lescaut, La Damnation de Faust, Tristan, Lohengrin, Tosca, Roméo et Juliette, and Fedora. But his favourite nights were the nights when Olive Fremstad sang. He heard her as Venus in Tannhäuser, as Selika in l'Africaine, as Carmen, and he heard her in that unique performance of Salome on January 22, 1907. One night he became so interested in watching her that he forgot to applaud the singer who had paid the claque. His delinquency was reported by one of his colleagues and the next evening, when he went to the bar on Seventh Avenue where the claque gathered to receive its orders, he was informed that his services would no longer be required.

After another three weeks of vagrancy, he found another job, again through a park acquaintance. He has told me that it was the only work he ever enjoyed. He became a "professor" in a house of pretty ladies. His duty was to play the piano. Play us another tune, professor, the customers would say, as they ordered beer at a dollar a bottle, and Peter would play a tune. Occasionally one of the customers would ask him to take a drink and he would order a sloe gin fizz, which Alonzo, the sick-looking waiter, a consumptive with a wife and five children to support, would bring in a sticky glass, which he deposited with his long dirty fingers on the ledge of the piano. Occasionally some man, waiting for a girl, was left alone with him, and would talk with him about the suspender business or the base-ball game, subjects which perhaps might not have interested him elsewhere but which glowed with an enthralling fire in that incongruous environment. The men preferred tunes like Lucia, the current Hippodrome success from Neptune's Daughter, or songs from The Red Mill, in which Montgomery and Stone were appearing at the Knickerbocker, or I don't care. This last was always demanded when a certain girl, who imitated Eva Tanguay, was in the room. But the women, when they were alone in the house, just before dinner in the late afternoon, or on a dull evening, always asked him to play Hearts and Flowers, Massenet's Elégie, or the garden scene from Faust, and then they would drink whisky and cry and tell him lies about their innocent girlhood. There was even some literary conversation. One of the girls read Georges Ohnet and another admired the work of Harris Merton Lyon and talked about it. Peter found it very easy to remain pure.

He received two dollars a night from the house, and, occasionally, tips. Out of this he managed to rent a hall bedroom on West Thirty-ninth Street and to pay for his lunches. The Madame provided him with his dinner. Breakfast he never ate. He passed his mornings in bed and his afternoons in the park, usually with a book.

A French girl named Blanche, whom he liked particularly, died one night. She was taken to a funeral chapel the next morning. The other girls went about the house snivelling and most of them sent flowers to the chapel. Blanche's coffin was well banked with carnations and tube-roses. The Madame sent a magnificent standing floral-piece, a cross of white roses and, on a ribbon, the inscription, May our darling rest in peace. Blanche wore a white lace dress and looked very beautiful and very innocent as she lay dead, Peter thought. Her mother came from a distant city and there was a priest. The two days preceding Blanche's burial, the girls passed in tears and prayers and sentimental remarks about how good she was. At night they worked as usual and Peter played the piano. It was very much like the Maison Tellier, he reflected.

With Peter, change was automatic and axiomatic, but he might have remained in the house a very long time, as he has assured me that he was perfectly contented, but for one of those accidents that never happen in realistic novels but which constantly happen in life. Mrs. Whiffle's brother, the graduate of Williams, erstwhile mentioned, a quaint person, who lived at Rochester, was a rich bachelor. He was also a collector, not of anything special, just a collector. He collected old andirons and doorknobs and knockers. He also collected postmarks and homespun coverlets and obsolete musical instruments. Occasionally he even collected books and in this respect his taste was unique. He collected first editions of Ouida, J. T. Trowbridge, Horatio Alger, Jr., G. A. Henty, and Oliver Optic. He had complete sets of first editions of all these authors and, unlike most book collectors, he read them with a great deal of pleasure. He especially enjoyed Cudjo's Cave, a novel he had devoured so many times that he had found it necessary to have the volume rebound, thus subtracting from its value if it ever comes up at an auction sale.

This uncle had always been prejudiced against Peter's father and, of late years, this prejudice had swollen into a first-rate aversion. Visits were never exchanged. He considered himself an amateur of parts and Peter's father, a sordid business grub. Mrs. Whiffle, however, whose whole nature was conciliatory, continued to write long letters to her brother. Recently she had turned to him for sympathy and had found a well of it. Mr. Fotheringay was ready to sympathize with anybody who had fled from old man Whiffle's tyranny. For the first time he began to take an interest in the boy whom he had never seen. His imagination fed on his sister's letters until it seemed to him that this boy was the only living being he had ever loved. Peter had been working among the daughters of joy about two months when Mr. Fotheringay died. When his will, made only a few weeks before his death, was read, it was discovered that he had left his collections to Williams College with the proviso that they be suitably housed, kept intact, and called the John Alden Fotheringay Collection. Williams College, I believe, was unable to meet the terms of the bequest and, as a result, through a contingent clause, they were sold. Not long ago, I ran across one of the books in Alfred F. Goldsmith's shop on Lexington Avenue in New York. It was a copy of J. T. Trowbridge's The Satin-Wood Box and it was easily identified by Mr. Fotheringay's bookplate, which represented an old man counting his gold, with the motto, In hoc signo vinces. After this department of the estate had been provided for in the will, a very considerable sum of money, well invested, remained. This was left to Peter without proviso.

As he never expected letters from any one except his mother, he seldom visited the post office and this particular communication from Mr. Fotheringay's lawyers, forwarded by Mrs. Whiffle, lay in a general delivery box for nearly a week before he called. He answered by telegraph and the next morning he received a substantial check at his hall bedroom address. The first thing he bought, he has told me, was a book, an extra-illustrated copy of Mademoiselle de Maupin, from Brentano's in Union Square. Then he went to a tailor and was measured for clothes. Next he visited Brooks Brothers, on Twenty-second Street and Broadway, and purchased a ready-made suit, a hat, shoes and stockings, shirts, and neckties. He took a bath, shaved, had his hair cut, and, dressed in his new finery, embarked for the Knickerbocker in a taxi. He walked into the bar under Maxfield Parrish's King Cole and ordered a Martini cocktail. Then he ate a dinner, consisting of terrapin, roast canvas-back, an alligator pear, and a quart or two of Pontet Canet. It was during the course of this dinner that it occurred to him, for the first time in his life, that he would become an author. Four days later he sailed for Paris.

VI

There is a considerable period in the life of George Borrow for which his biographers have been absolutely unable to account. To this day where Borrow spent those lost years is either unknown or untold. There is a similar period in the life of Peter Whiffle, the period including the years 1907–1913. In the summer of the former year I left him at Paris in the arms of Clara Barnes, so to speak, and I did not see him again until February, 1913. Subsequently, when I knew him better, I inquired about these phantom years but I never elicited a satisfactory reply. He answered me, to be sure, but his answer consisted of two words, I lived.

Our next meeting took place in New York, where I was a musical reporter on the New York Times, the assistant to Mr. Richard Aldrich. One night, having dropped Fania Marinoff at the theatre where she was playing, I walked south-east until I came to the Bowery. I strolled down that decaying thoroughfare, which has lost much of its ancient glory—even the thugs and the belles of Avenue A have deserted it—to Canal Street, where the Manhattan Bridge invites the East Side to adventure through its splendid portal, but the East Side ignores the invitation and stays at home. It is the upper West Side that accepts the invitation and regiments of motor-cars from Riverside Drive, in continuous procession, pass over the bridge. For a time I stood and watched the ugly black scarabs with their acetylene eyes crawl up the approach and disappear through the great arch and then, walking a few steps, I stopped before the Thalia Theatre, as I have stopped so many times, to admire the noble façade with its flight of steps and its tall columns, for this is one of my dream theatres. Often have I sat in the first row of the dress circle, which is really a circle, leaning over the balustrade, gazing into the pit a few feet below, and imagining the horseshoe as it might appear were it again frequented by the fashion of the town. This is a theatre, in which, and before which, it has often amused me to fancy myself a man of wealth, when my first diversion would be a complete renovation—without any reconstruction or vandalism—of this playhouse, and the production of some play by Shakespeare, for to me, no other theatre in New York, unless it be the Academy of Music, lends itself so readily to a production of Shakespeare as the Thalia. As I write these lines, I recall that the old New York theatres are fast disappearing: Wallack's is gone; Daly's is no more; even Weber and Fields's has been demolished. Cannot something be done to save the Thalia, which is much older than any of these? Cannot this proud auditorium be reconsecrated to the best in the drama? On this night I paused for a moment, musing before the portal, somewhat after this manner—for I have always found that *things* rather than people awaken any latent sentiment and sympathy in my heart—and then again I passed on.

Soon I came to a tiny Chinese shop, although I was still several blocks above Chinatown. The window was stacked with curious crisp waffles or wafers in the shape of lotus flowers, for the religious and sexual symbolism of the Chinese extends even to their culinary functions, and a Chinaman, just inside, was dexterously transferring the rice batter to the irons, which were placed over the fire, turned a few moments, and a wafer removed and sprinkled with dry rice powder, as Richelieu, lacking a blotter, sprinkled pounce on his wet signature. But the shop was not consecrated solely to the manufacture of waffles; there were tea-sets and puppy-cats, all the paraphernalia of a Chinese shop in New York—on the shelves and tables. It was the waffles, and the peanut cakes, however, which tempted me to enter.

Once inside, I became aware of the presence of a Chinese woman at the back of the shop, holding in her arms an exquisite Chinese baby, for all Chinese babies, with their flat porcelain faces, their straight black hair, and their ivory hands, are exquisite. This baby, in green-blue trousers fashioned of some soft silk brocade, a pink jacket of the same material, and a head-dress prankt with ribbons into which ornaments of scarlet worsted and blue-bird feathers were twisted, was smiling silently and gracefully waving her tiny ivory hands towards the face of an outcast of the streets who stood beside her mother. I caught the rough workman's suit, the soiled, torn boots, the filthy cap, and the unkempt hair in my glance, which reverted to the baby. Then, as I approached the odd group, and spoke to the mother, the derelict turned.

Carl! he exclaimed, for, of course, it was Peter.

I was too much astonished to speak at all, as I stared at this ragged figure without a collar or a tie, with several days growth of beard on his usually glabrous cheeks, and dirty finger-nails. I had only wit enough left to shake his hand. At this time I knew nothing of his early life, nothing of the fortune he had inherited, and the man in front of me, save for something curiously inconsistent in the expression of the face, was a tramp. Certainly the face was puzzling: it positively exuded happiness. Perhaps, I thought, it was because he was glad to see me. I was glad to see him, even in this guise.

Carl, he repeated, dear old Carl! How silly of me not to remember that you would be in New York. He caught my glance. Somewhat of a change, eh? No more ruffles and frills. That life, and everything connected with it, is finished. Luckily, you've caught me near home. Come with me; there's liquor there.

So we walked out. I had not yet spoken a word. I was choking with an emotion I usually reserve for old theatres, but Peter did not appear to be aware of it. He chattered on gaily.

Have you been to Paris recently? Where have you been? What have you been doing? Are you writing? Isn't New York lovely? Don't you think Chinese babies are the kind to have, if you are going to become a father at all? Wasn't that an adorable one? He waited for no answers. Look at the lights on the bridge. I live in the shadow of the span. I think I live somewhere near the old Five Points that used to turn up in all the old melodramas; you know, The Streets of New York. It's a wonderful neighbourhood. Everybody, absolutely *everybody*, is interesting. There's nobody you can't talk to, and very few that can't talk. They all have something to say. They are all either disappointed and discouraged or hopeful. They all have emotions and they are not afraid to show them. They all talk about the REVOLUTION. It may come this winter. No, I don't mean the Russian revolution. Nobody expects a revolution in Russia. Nobody down here is interested in Russia; the Russian Jews especially are not. They have forgotten Russia. I mean the American REVOLUTION. The Second American REVOLUTION, I suppose it will be called. Labour against Capital. The Workman against the Leisure Class. The Proletariat against the Idler. Did you ever hear of Piet Vlag? Do you read The Masses? I go to meetings, union meetings, Socialist meetings, I. W. W. meetings, Syndicalist meetings, Anarchist meetings. I egg them on. It may come this winter, I tell you! There will be barricades on Fifth Avenue. Vanderbilt and Rockefeller will be besieged in their houses with the windows shuttered and the doors barred and the butler standing guard with a machine-gun at some gazebo or turret. It will be a real siege, lasting, perhaps, months. How long will the food hold out? In the end, they'll have to eat the canary and the Pekinese, and, no, not the cat, I hope. The cat will be clever and escape, go over to the enemy where he can get his meals. But boots, boot soup! Just like the siege of Paris; each robber baron locked up in his stronghold. Sometimes, the housemaid will desert; sometimes, the cook. The millionaires will be obliged to make their own beds and cook their own dogs and, at last, to man their own machine-guns!

The mob will be barricaded, too, behind barriers hastily thrown up in the street, formed of old moving-vans, Rolls-Royces and Steinway grands, covered with Gobelin tapestries and Lilihan, Mosul, Sarouk, and Khorassan rugs, the spoils of the denuded houses. With a red handkerchief bound around my brow, I will wave a red flag and shriek on the top of such a barricade. My face will be streaked with blood. We will all yell and if we don't sing the Ça Ira and the Carmagnole, we will at least sing Alexander's Ragtime Band and My Wife's Gone to the Country.

Eventually, Fifth Avenue will fall and the Astors and the Goulds will be brought before the Tribunal of the People, and if you know any better spot for a guillotine than the very square in which we stood just now, in that vast open space before the Manhattan Bridge, over which they all drive off for Long Island, I wish you'd tell me. There are those who would like to see the killing done in Washington or Madison Square, or the Plaza or Columbus Circle, which, of course, has a sentimental interest for the Italians, but think of the joy it would give the East Side mothers, suckling their babies, and the pushcart vendors, and all the others who never find time to go up town to have the show right here. Right here it shall be, if I have my way, and just now I have a good deal of influence.

We had stopped before one of those charming old brick houses with marble steps and ancient hand-wrought iron railings which still remain on East Broadway to remind us of the day when stately landaus drove up to deposit crinolined ladies before their portals. We ascended the steps and Peter opened the door with his key. The hallway was dark but Peter struck matches to light us up the stairs and we only ceased climbing when we reached the top landing. He unlocked another door which opened on a spacious chamber, a lovely old room with a chaste marble fire-place in the Dorian mode, and faded wall-paper of rose and grey, depicting Victorian Greek females, taller than the damsels drawn by Du Maurier and C. D. Gibson, languishing in the shadows of broken columns and weeping willow trees. Upon this paper were fastened with pins a number of covers from radical periodicals, native and foreign, some in vivid colours, the cover of The Masses for March, 1912, Charles A. Winter's Enlightenment versus Violence, the handsome head of a workman, his right hand bearing a torch, printed in green, several cartoons by Art Young, usually depicting the rich man as an octopus or hog, and posters announcing meetings of various radical groups. Gigantic letters, cut from sheets of newspaper, formed the legend, I. W. W., over the door.

The room was almost devoid of furniture. There was an iron bed, with tossed bed-clothing, a table on which lay a few books, including, I noted, one by Karl Marx, another by English Walling, Frank Harris's The Bomb, together with a number of copies of Piet Vlag's new journal, The Masses, and Jack Marinoff's Yiddish comic weekly, The Big Stick. There was also a pail on the table, such a pail as that in which a workman carries his mid-day meal. There were exactly two chairs and a wardrobe of polished oak in the best Grand Rapids manner stood in one corner. All this was sufficiently bewildering but I must confess that the appearance of the lovely head of a Persian cat, issuing from under the bed-covers, made me doubt my reason. I recognized George Moore. Presently I made out another puss, sitting beside a basket full of kittens in the corner near the wardrobe.

I must introduce you, explained Peter, to the mother of George Moore's progeny. This is George Sand.

By this time I was a fit subject for the asylum. Even the Persian cats did not set me right. Happy or not, the man was evidently poor.

I suppose I would insult you if I offered you a job, I stuttered at last.

A job! Carl, don't you know that I simply will not work?

Well, and I found this even more difficult than my first proposal, I hope you won't misunderstand. . . I haven't much. . . but you must permit me to give you some money.

Money! What for?

Why, for you. . .

Comprehending at last, Peter threw back his head and began to laugh.

But I don't need money. . . I never had so little use for it. Do you realize what it costs me to live here? About $15 a week. That includes every item, even fresh beef for my cats. I was about to tell you, if you had given me time—you always interrupt—that I simply don't know what to do with my money. Stocks have gone up. The labourers in the factories at Little Falls are working overtime to make me more prosperous. Indeed, one of the reasons I was so glad to see you was that I thought, perhaps, you could help me to spend some money.

The line about the interruptions, I should explain, was simply a fabrication of Peter's. If I have set our conversations down as monologues on his part, that is just how they occurred. Aside from Philip Moeller and Arnold Daly, I have never known any one to talk so much, and my rôle with Peter, as with them, was that of listener. To continue, I should have known enough, even so early in our acquaintance, not to be astonished by anything he might do, but if there had been a mirror in the room, which there was not, I fancy I might have looked into the most exasperatingly astonished face I had ever seen up to that time. I managed, however, to laugh. Peter laughed, too, and sat down. George Moore leaped to his knee and George Sand to his shoulder, rubbing her magnificent orange brush across his face.

And how about your book? I asked.

It's coming. . . coming fast.

Are you still collecting notes?

Notes? . . . O! you are remembering what I was doing in Paris. *That* was only an experiment. . . I was on the wrong track. . . I threw them all away! I couldn't do anything with *that*. . . I'm done with such nonsense.

I couldn't be astonished any more.

What are you doing now?

I've told you. I'm *living*. O! I'm full of it: I know what art is now; I know what real literature is. It has nothing to do with style or form or manner. George Moore, not my cat but the other one, has said that Christianity is not a stranger religion than the cult of the inevitable word. The *matter* is what counts. I think it was Theodore Dreiser. . .

Here I did interrupt:

I know him. When I first came to New York in 1906, I wrote a paper about Richard Strauss's Salome for the Broadway Magazine. He was the editor.

You know Theodore Dreiser!

There was awe in his tone.

Very slightly. I saw something of him then. Principally, I remember his habit, when he was talking, of folding his handkerchief into small squares, then unfolding it. He repeated this process indefinitely.

Show me.

I showed him.

Well, I'm glad I met you tonight. . . It was Sister Carrie that set me right; at least I think it was Sister Carrie. What a book! What a masterpiece! No style, no form, just *subject*. The devils flogged

St. Jerome in the fifth century because he was rather a Ciceronian than a Christian in his beautiful writing, but they never will flog Theodore Dreiser! He had an idea, he knew life, and he just wrote what he felt. He wasn't thinking of *how* to write it; he had something to write. Have you read Sister Carrie?

I explained that Edna Kenton had given me the book to read when it first appeared.

Strange as it may appear to you, for my way is not, perhaps, Dreiser's, that book explains why I am here and why I dress in this manner. It explains why I wander about the streets and talk with the people. It explains why I am hoping for the REVOLUTION (Peter on this occasion invariably pronounced this word in capitals). It explains why I am an I. W. W. I would even join the Elks, if necessary. I think Dreiser at one time must have been an Elk; else how could he describe Hurstwood so perfectly?

It is amusing, however, that you who won't work should become an international worker!

I dare say it is, drawled Peter, stroking George Moore's back, as the superb cat lay purring on his knee. I dare say it is but I'd go a good deal farther to get what I want; I'd even seek employment in a department store or a Chinese laundry. However, it's coming without that, it's coming fast. I found my heroine the other day, a little Jewish girl, who works in a sweat-shop. She has one blue eye and one black one. She has a club-foot, a hare-lip, and she is a hunch-back. I nearly cried for joy when I discovered her. I met her on Rivington Street walking with a stack of men's overcoats three feet high poised on her head. She was limping under her burden. I followed her to the shop and made some inquiries. Her name is Rosie Levenstein. I shall leave in the deformities, but I shall change her name.

Isn't she just a trifle unpleasant, a little unsympathetic, for a heroine?

My book, replied Peter, is going to be very unpleasant. It is about life and because you and I enjoy life is little enough reason for us to consider it other than a dirty business. Life for the average person, for Rosie, for instance, simply will not do. It's bloody awful and, if anything, I shall make it worse than it is. Now, if the comrades succeed in starting the REVOLUTION, I am going through with it, straight through, breaking into drawingrooms with the others. I'm going to pound up a Steinway grand with a hammer. Here Peter, with a suitable gesture, brought his hand down rather heavily on George Moore's head and that one, indignant, immediately rose and jumped down from his lap, subsequently stretched himself on the floor, catching his claws in the carpet, and after yawning once or twice, retreated under the bed. George Sand now left Peter's shoulder to fill the vacant place on his knee. As I told you, I'm going to wear a red handkerchief round my brow and my face will be bloody. Then, all I have to do is to transfer the whole experience, everything *I* have done and felt, the thrill, the BOOM, to Rosie. Can't you see the picture in my last chapter of the little, lame, harelipped hunch-back, with one blue eye and one black one, marching up Fifth Avenue with the comrades, wrapped in the red flag, her face stained with blood, humbling the Guggenheimers and the Morgans, disturbing the sleep of Henry Clay Frick, casting art treasures, bought with the blood of the poor, out to the pavement, breaking windows, shooting, torturing, devastating? Then the triumphant return to the East Side, Rosie on the men's shoulders. Everybody tired and sweaty, satiated and bloody. Now, all the realism of the interiors, gefillte fish and schnaps. But Rosie will sit down to her dinner in a Bendel evening gown, raped from one of the Kahn closets. The men come back for her. Another procession down Canal Street. The police charge the mob. Shots. The Vanderbilts and the Astors and the Schwabs in their Rolls-Royces and their Pierce-Arrows, fitted with machine-guns, charge the mob. Terrible slaughter. Rosie dead, a horrid mess, fully described, lying on the pavement. Everything lost. Everything worse than it was before. Deportation. Exile. Tenements razed. Old women, their sheitels awry, wrapped in half a dozen petticoats and thick shawls, bearing the sacred candlesticks, fleeing in all directions. Cries of Weh is mir! Moans. Groans. Desolation. And, at the end, a lone figure standing just where you and I were standing a little while ago, philosophizing, pointing the dread moral, accenting the horror. The lights go out. Darkness. In the distance, a band is heard playing The Star Spangled Banner. Finis.

Peter's excitement became so great that he almost shrieked; he waved his arms and he half rose out of his chair. George Sand, too, found it expedient to retreat under the bed. The kittens, tumbling mewing out of their baskets, their little tails, like Christmas trees, straight in the air, followed her, and soon were pushing their paws valiantly against her belly and drinking greedily from her dugs.

It's wonderful, I said when Peter, at last, was silent. Then, as it seemed, rather inconsequentially, Do you know Edith Dale?

Who is Edith Dale?

Well, she's a woman, but a new kind of woman, or else the oldest kind; I'm not sure which. I'm going to take you there. Bill Haywood goes there. So does Doris Keane. Everybody goes there. Everything is all mixed up. Everybody talks his own kind of talk and Edith, inscrutable Edith, sits back and listens. You can listen too.

Is she writing a book?

No, she never does anything like that. She spends her energy in living, in watching other people live, in watching them make their silly mistakes, in helping them make their silly mistakes. She is a dynamo. She will give you a good deal. At least, these gatherings will give you a good deal. I think you might carry a chapter or two of your novel through one of Edith Dale's evenings.

Must I change my clothes?

No, you are right just as you are. She will like you the better for them.

That's good. I couldn't change my clothes. My friends, the comrades, wouldn't understand if they saw me. But you must have a drink. I had nearly forgotten that I had promised you one:

Peter opened the polished oak wardrobe and extracted therefrom a bottle of Christopher's Finest Old White Scotch Whisky and he began to speak of the advantage of allowing spirits to retain their natural colour, which rarely happens in the case of whisky, although gin is ordinarily to be distinguished in this manner.

VII

E dith Dale had returned to New York after three years in Florence. Near the old renaissance city, she had purchased an ancient villa in the mountains and had occupied herself during her sojourn there in transforming it into a perfect environment for the amusing people with whom she surrounded herself. The villa originally had been built without a loggia; this was added, together with a salone in the general style of the old house. The lovely Italian garden was restored. Cypresses pointed their dark green cones towards the sky and gardenias bloomed. White peacocks and statues were imported. Then, with her superlatively excellent taste at her elbow, Edith rushed about Italy in her motor, ravishing prie-Dieu, old pictures, fans, china dogs, tapestries, majolica, and Capo di Monte porcelains, carved and gilded renaissance boxes, fantastic Venetian glass girandoles, refectory tables, divans, and divers bibelots, until the villa became a perfect expression of her mood. When every possible accent had been added, she entertained in the evening. Eleanora Duse, a mournful figure in black velvet, stood on the loggia and gazed out over the hills towards Certosa; Gordon Craig postured in the salone; and Gertrude Stein commemorated the occasion in a pamphlet, printed and bound in a Florentine floral wallpaper, which today fetches a good sum in old bookshops, when it can be found at all. To those present at this festa, it seemed, doubtless, like the inauguration of the reign of another Lorenzo the Magnificent. There was, indeed, the prospect that Ease and Grace, Beauty, Wit, and Knowledge, would stroll through these stately and ornate chambers for indefinite months, while hungry artists were being fed in the diningroom. But to Edith, this culminating dreary festivity was the end. She had decorated her villa with its last china dog, and the greatest actress in the world was standing on her loggia. Under the circumstances, further progress in this direction seemed impossible. She was even somewhat chagrined to recall that it had taken her three years to accomplish these things and she resolved to move more quickly in the future. So, packing enough of her treasures to furnish an apartment in New York, she shut the villa door without looking behind her, and booked a passage on the next boat sailing from Genoa.

In New York she found the top floor of an old mansion in Washington Square exactly what she wanted and installed green glass, lovely fabrics, and old Italian furniture against the ivory-white of the walls and the hangings. She accomplished the setting in a week; now she required the further decoration which the human element would afford. Art, for the moment, was her preoccupation and, with her tremendous energy and her rare sagacity and taste, she set about, quite spontaneously, arranging for an exhibition, the first great exhibition of the post-impressionist and cubist painters in New York. This show has now become almost a legend but it was the reality of that winter. It was the first, and possibly the last, exhibition of paintings held in New York which everybody attended. Everybody went and everybody talked about it. Street-car conductors asked for your opinion of the Nude Descending the Staircase, as they asked you for your nickel. Elevator boys grinned about Matisse's Le Madras Rouge, Picabia's La Danse à la Source, and Brancusi's Mademoiselle Pogany, as they lifted you to the twenty-third floor. Ladies, you met at dinner, found Archipenko's sculpture very amusing, but was it art? Alfred Stieglitz, whose 291 Gallery had nourished similar ideas for years, spouted like a geyser for three weeks and then, after a proper interval, like Old Faithful, began again. Actresses began to prefer Odilon Redon to Raphael Kirchner. To sum up, the show was a bang-up, whale of a success, quite overshadowing the coeval appearance of the Irish Players, chaperoned by Lady Gregory. It was cartooned, it was caricatured, it was Dr. Frank Craned. Scenes in the current revues at the theatres were devoted to it; it was even mentioned in a burlesque at the Columbia. John Wanamaker advertised cubist gowns and ladies began to wear green, blue, and violet wigs, and to paint their faces emerald and purple. The effects of this æsthetic saturnalia are manifest even today.

Fresh from the quieter insanity of Florence, Edith was intensely amused by all this. It seemed so extraordinarily droll to find the great public awake to the excitement of art. She surrounded herself with as many storm centres as possible. The crowds flocked to her place and she made them comfortable. Pinchbottles and Curtis Cigarettes, poured by the hundreds from their neat pine boxes into white bowls, trays of Virginia ham and white Gorgonzola sandwiches, pale Italian boys in aprons, and a Knabe piano were added to the decorations. Arthur Lee and Lee Simonson, Marsden Hartley, Andrew Dasburg, Max Weber, Charles Demuth, Bobby Jones—just out of college and not yet a designer of scenery—, Bobby Parker, all the jeunes were confronted with dowagers from the upper East Side, old family friends, Hutchins

Hapgood, Ridgely Torrence, Edwin Arlington Robinson, and pretty women. Arguments and discussions floated in the air, were caught and twisted and hauled and tied, until the white salon itself was no longer static. There were undercurrents of emotion and sex.

Edith was the focus of the group, grasping this faint idea or that frail theory, tossing it back a complete or wrecked formula, or she sat quietly with her hands folded, like a Madonna who had lived long enough to learn to listen. Sometimes she was not even at home, for the drawing-room was generally occupied from ten in the morning until midnight. Sometimes—very often, indeed—, she left her guests without a sign and went to bed. Sometimes—and this happened still oftener—, she remained in the room, without being present. Andrew Dasburg commemorated this aspect in a painting which he called The Absence of Edith Dale. But always, and Dasburg suggested this in his flame-like portrait, her electric energy presided. She was the amalgam which held the incongruous group together; she was the alembic that turned the dross to gold.

When dulness, beating its tiresome wings, seemed about to hover over the group, she had a habit of introducing new elements into the discussion, or new figures into the group itself, and one day it must have occurred to her that, if people could become so excited about art, they might be persuaded to become excited about themselves too, and so she transferred her interest to the labouring man, to unions, to strikes, to the I. W. W. I remember the first time I saw her talking earnestly with a rough member of the garment-maker's union. Two days later, Bill Haywood, himself, came in and the tremendous presence of the one-eyed giant filled the room, seeming to give it a new consecration. Débutantes knelt on the floor beside him, while he talked simply, but with an enthralling intensity, about the things that interested him, reinforcing his points by crushing the heels of his huge boots into the Shirvan rug or digging his great hands into the mauve tapestry with which the divan was upholstered. Miners, garment-workers, and silk-weavers were the honoured guests in those days. The artists still came but the centre of interest had shifted. Almost half of every day, Edith now spent in Paterson, New Jersey, where the strike of the hour was going on, attending union meetings and helping to carry pickets back and forth in her motor. She continued to be diverted by the ironies and complexities of life.

Recruits to the circle arrived from Europe—for Edith knew half of Europe—; solemn celebrities, tramps, upper Fifth Avenue, Gramercy

Park, Greenwich Village, a few actresses—I took Fania Marin-off there several times—were all mixed up with green glass vases, filled with fragrant white lilies, salmon snapdragons, and blue larkspurs, pinchbottles, cigarette stubs, Lincoln Steffens, and the paintings of Marsden Hartley and Arthur B. Davies. Over the whole floated the dominant odours of Coty's chypre and stale beer.

Edith herself was young—about thirty-four—and comely, with a face that could express anything or nothing more easily than any face I have ever seen. It was a perfect mask. She wore lovely gowns of clinging turquoise blue, spinel, and jacinth silks from Liberty's. When she went out, she wrapped herself in more soft silks of contrasting shades, and donned such a hat as Donatello's David wears, graceful with its waving plumes and an avalanche of drooping veils.

I spent whole days at Edith's and was nearly as much amused as she. To be truthful, I dare say I was more amused, because she tired of it before I did. But before these days were over I brought in Peter. I had telephoned Edith that we were coming for dinner and, when we arrived, the rooms were nearly empty, for she found it as easy to rid herself of people as to gather them in. Neith Boyce was there, I remember, her lovely red hair caught in a low knot and her lithe body swathed in a deep blue brocade. There were two young men whose names I never knew, for Edith never introduced anybody and these young men did not interest me sufficiently to compel me to converse with them and they interested Edith so little that they were never allowed to appear again. The dinner, as always, was simple: a soup, roast beef and browned potatoes, peas, a salad of broccoli, a loaf of Italian bread, pats of sweet butter, and cheese and coffee. Bottles of whisky, red and white wine, and beer stood at intervals along the unclothed refectory table. The cynical Tuscan butler, who had once been in the service of Lady Paget, never interrupted the meals to serve these. You poured out what you wanted when you wanted it. The dinner was dull. The young men tried to make an impression on Edith, with a succession of witty remarks of the sort which would have made them exceedingly popular in anything like what Ward McAllister describes as Society as I Have Found It, but it was apparent that their hostess was unaware of their very existence. Neith and I exchanged a few inconsequential phrases concerning D. H. Lawrence's Sons and Lovers. Peter, dressed as he had been when I met him in the Chinese shop, and even dirtier, was utterly silent. Long before coffee was served, Edith left the table and went into the salon to write letters.

When we followed her later, there were already a few people there, talking in corners, and more were arriving. Now and again, Edith glanced up from her letters to greet one of the newcomers but she did not rise. Peter wandered about the room, looking at the pictures, occasionally picking up a book, of which there were a great number lying about on the tables. Donald Evans, correct and rather portentous in his studied dignity, made an early appearance. At this period he was involved in the composition of the Sonnets from the Patagonian. He drew a manuscript from his pocket and laid it on the desk before Edith. Over her shoulder I read the line,

She triumphed in the tragic turnip field.

Hutchins Hapgood, haggard and restless and yet strangely sympathetic, came in and joined uneasily in an eager conversation with a young woman with bobbed hair who stood in a corner, fingering an African primitive carving in wood of a naked woman with long pointed breasts. Yorska was there, the exotic Yorska with her long nose, her tragic eyes, her mouth like a crimson slit in a face as white as Pierrot's, a modern Judith looking for a modern Holofernes and never finding him; Jo Davidson with his jovial black beard, Bacchus or satyr in evening clothes; Edna Kenton, in a pale green floating tunic of her own design; Max Eastman, poet and Socialist, and his wife, Ida Rauh; Helen Westley, a tall angular scrag with something of the aristocracy of the Remsen-Meseroles informing her spine, who had acquired a considerable reputation for being "paintable" by never paying the slightest attention to her clothes; Henrietta Rodman, the round-faced, cherubic Max Weber. . . I caught all these and, quite suddenly, although for some time, I remembered afterward, I had been aware of the odour of Cœur de Jeannette, Clara Barnes. She was sitting, when I discovered her, on a sofa before the fire-place, in which the coals were glowing. She was more matronly in figure and was dressed with some attempt at stylization. She was wearing a robe of batik, iridescent in the shades of the black opal, with a belt of moonstones set in copper, and huge earrings fashioned of human hair. On her feet were copper-coloured sandals and I was pleased to note that her dress was long enough to cover her ankles. I leaned over the back of the sofa and addressed her,

Miss Barnes, I believe. . .

She turned.

Oh, it's you. What a long time it's been since Paris.

I perceived that her new manner was not exclusively a matter of clothes.

Peter is here tonight, I hazarded.

Is he? she parried, without any apparent interest.

What are you doing now?

What I have always been doing, studying for opera. That teacher in Paris nearly ruined my voice. I am really, it seems, a contralto, and that fool had me studying Manon. Carmen is to be my great rôle. I have a splendid teacher now and I am working hard. In two or three more years, I should be ready for my début. I want to get into the Metropolitan. . . You, I hear, are with the Times. Perhaps you can help me. . .

So she rambled on. I had heard everything she had to say many times before and I have heard it many times since; I found it hard to listen. Looking across the room, I saw Peter gazing at us. So he knew she was there, but he only smiled and turned back his attention to the book he held in his hand. Clara, however, had caught his eye. Her face became hard and bitter.

He might speak to me, she said and there was a tone of defiance in her voice. Then, more calmly, I never understood Peter; I don't understand him now. For three days, a week, perhaps, I thought he loved me. One day he disappeared, without any explanation; nothing, not a sign, not a word. I knew that he had left Paris, because he had taken the cat with him. I was not very much in love with him and so it didn't hurt, at least it didn't hurt deeply, but what do you make of a man like that?

He contradicts himself, I put in rather lamely, searching for words.

That's it! He contradicts himself. Why, do you know, I don't believe he cared at all for my singing. After the day I sang for you, he never asked me to sing again and when I offered to he always put me off.

An old lady in a black satin dress, trimmed with cataracts of jet beads, addressed me and fortunately drew me out of Clara's orbit.

Mrs. Dale has some remarkable pictures of the new school, she began, but, of course, I don't like them. Now, if you want to see pictures—I hadn't said that I did—you should go to Henry Frick's. Do you know Mr. Frick?

No, but I know the man who shot him.

The old lady grew almost apoplectic and the jet beads jangled like Æolian harps in a heavy wind. She managed, however, to gasp out with a sound that was remarkably like gurgling, O! indeed! How interesting! Then, peering about nervously, I don't suppose he's here tonight.

I haven't seen him, I said, but he often comes here and, as I see Emma Goldman yonder, I should think it extremely likely that he will appear later.

O! indeed! The old lady leitmotived once more, How interesting! How very interesting! Would you mind telling me the time?

It's a quarter of ten.

O! As late as that!—She had just arrived. Really, I had no idea it was so late. John—this to a decrepit old gentleman in shiny evening clothes—, John, it's a quarter to ten.

What of it? querulously demanded the old gentleman, with a curious upward turn to his ridiculous side-whiskers. What of it?

The old lady, forgetting her fifty years of training in the most exclusive drawing-rooms, turned and whispered something in his ear.

Now it was the turn of the old gentleman to feel a touch of apoplexy.

Berkman! he roared, Berkman! Where is the scoundrel? Where is the assassin?

The old lady looked almost shame-faced as she tried to pacify John: He's not here yet, but he may come.

We shall leave at once, announced the old gentleman decisively. Edith is trespassing on our good nature. She is going too far. We shall leave at once.

He offered the old lady his arm and they made their way rapidly out, rubbing against, in the passageway, a one-eyed man nearly seven feet tall. Now Edith had neither observed the coming or the going of this elderly couple but Bill Haywood had not crossed the threshold before she was shaking his hand and, a moment later, she had drawn him with her through a doorway into a little room at one side of the salon, where she could talk to him more privately.

The most fascinating man alive, volunteered a stranger at my elbow, a little fellow with a few wisps of yellow hair and a face like a pug-dog, that Bill Haywood. No show about him, nothing theatrical, not a bit like the usual labour leader. Genuine power, that's what he has. He never goes in for melodrama, not even at a strike meeting. The other day in Paterson, a child was hurt while the police were clearing the street of strikers. One of the policemen, with his billy, struck down the boy's mother and a man who was helping her to her feet. At the meeting the next day, Haywood recited the facts, just the bare facts, without comment or colour and without raising his voice. What's the policeman's name? cried a voice in the hall. His name, replied Haywood, as coldly as possible, is said to be Edward Duffy; his number is 72. That was all, but Edward Duffy, No 72, had been consigned to the perpetual hatred of every one of the two thousand men present at the meeting. He spurns eloquence and soap-box platitudes. He never gibbers about the brotherhood of man, the socialist commonwealth rising upon the ruins of the capitalist system, death to the exploiters, and all the other clichés of the ordinary labour agitator. Workers want simple, homely facts regarding their trades and he gives them these facts. He is—

What are all these God damn bourgeois doing here? demanded a high, shrill voice from the next room.

My companion smiled. That is Hippolyte Havel. He always asks that question, even at anarchist meetings, but it isn't a cliché with him; it's part of his charm.

Hippolyte, sweet, blinking, amblyoptic Hippolyte, his hair as snarly as the Medusa's, strode into the room.

Hush, some one adjured us, Hush! Yorska is going to recite.

After a few seconds, there was silence. All the chairs were filled; many were sitting on the floor or standing against the wall or in the doorways; ladies in black velvet, wearing diamonds, ladies in batik and Greenwich village sacks, ladies with bobbed hair and mannish-cut garments, men in evening dress, men in workmen's clothes. No one present, I noted, looked quite so untidy as Peter. Yorska, her tragic face emerging from three yards of black tulle and satin, recited, in French, Baudelaire's Le Balcon, fingering a red rose at her waist. As she uttered the last lines with passionate intensity,

—O serments! O parfums! O baisers infinis!

there was a scattered clapping of hands, a few exclamations of delight. Now the Tuscan butler, as cynical as Herbert Spencer, threw open the doors to the dining-room, exposing the table laden with sandwiches, salads, cold meats, glasses, and bottles, including kümmel bottles in the form of Russian bears. A few of the young radicals were the first to surge to the repast. My companion and I slipped out in time to hear an instructive lecture on the subject of collective bargaining from a young man with a black flowing tie, who grasped a pinchbottle so fervidly that I felt sure it would never leave his hand until he had usurped the contents. Representation was a word which, in its different senses, was often used that evening. The labourers cooed over it, worshipped it, and set it up in a shrine, while the artists spurned it and cast it from them; "mere photography" was the phrase.

Helen Westley, black and limp, stood beside me.

Who, she asked, is that young man you brought here tonight?

Peter Whiffle, I replied.

Peter Whistle? was her interrogative reproduction.

Presently the quiet even voice of Bill Haywood was heard from the drawing-room, a voice that by its very mildness compelled silence:

Violence, yes, we advocate violence of the most violent sort, violence that consists in keeping your mouth shut and your hands in your pockets. Don't fold your arms, I say to the men, but keep your hands in your pockets to keep hired thugs and detectives from putting bombs there. In doing this and staying on strike you are committing the most violent acts in the world, for you are stopping industry and keeping it stopped until the mill owners grant your demands, an eight hour day, two looms to a worker, and higher wages.

See how he talks, pointed out my unidentified companion, rubbing his flabby fingers the while around the flange of his wine-glass, about half-full of red California wine. No rage, no emotion, a simple explanation of the humanities. Let us go in where we can hear him better.

But when we joined the throng in the drawing-room, we discovered that Haywood was not beginning. He had already finished what he had to say to the group and had returned to his more intimate conversation with Edith. He brought back to my mind Cunninghame Graham's description of Parnell, not popular, in the hail-fellow-well-met and loudly cheered conception of the word, but yet with an attraction for all women whom he came across, who were drawn to him by his careless treatment of them, and by the wish that nature has implanted in their sex, to be the rulers of all men who stand above their kind.

Did it ever occur to you? my companion began again, that there is some strange relationship between trade unionism and tribal magic? You know how the men of one union cannot do the work for the men of another union. What is this restriction but the taboo?

What, indeed? I echoed pleasantly, unable to think of anything more apposite to say. Besides, my attention was wandering. I had discovered Peter, who appeared to be engrossed in the charms of a pretty girl of whom I knew little except that her name was Mahalah Wiggins.

CARL VAN VECHTEN

Now the round-faced, cherubic Max Weber rose to speak.

The art consciousness is the great life consciousness, he began in his somewhat high-pitched voice. Its product and the appreciation of its product are the very flower of life. . . Hutchins Hapgood's companion continued to finger lovingly the polished wooden African figure. . . Its presence in man is Godliness on earth. It humanizes mankind. Were it spread broadcast it would do away with dry, cold intellectualism, which dead and unfired, always seeks refuge in pretending to be more than it is. . . Bill Haywood, the giant Arimaspian, was pounding the seat of the brocaded sofa with his great fist. . . Art or art consciousness is the real proof of genuine human sympathy. It oozes spiritual expression. Were it fostered it would sooner solve the great modern economic problem than any labour propaganda. . . Helen Westley was yawning, with a great open jaw, which she made no effort to conceal. . . A lack of this art consciousness—Weber was very earnest, but in no sense theatrical—, on the part of both capital and labour, is one cause of this great modern struggle. Were this art consciousness more general, material possession would be less valued; the covetous spirit would soon die out. . . Yorska, a wraith of black satin and black tulle, her pale Pierrot face slit with crimson and punctuated with two black holes, lined with purple, stood in the doorway motionless, like another Rachel, with one hand lifted above her head, grasping the curtain, trying to look uncovetous. . . Art socializes more than socialism with its platform and its platitudes. . . Bravo! This from Hippolyte Havel. . . Economists go not deep enough into the modern monetary disease. They deal only with materialism. They concentrate only on what is obvious, the physical starvation of the toiling class, but never do they see or seem to realize the spiritual starvation or the lack of an art consciousness to both capital and labour. They would argue that the material relief must come first. I reply, now as always, we must begin with the spiritual. I do not see, however, how the spiritual or æsthetic can be separated from the material. . . Clara Barnes gave an angry shake to her long earrings, but Donald Evans had the rapt attentive air of a man hearing a great truth for the first time. . . The common solution of this great problem is too dry, too matter of fact, too calculated, too technical, too scientifically intellectual and not enough intellectually imaginative. Art consciousness is not merely a form of etiquette, nor a phase of culture—it is life—the quality of sensitive breathing, seeing, hearing, developed to a high true spirituality. Man would value man more. The wonder of and the faith in other human beings would kindle a new social and spiritual life.

That's good talk, was Bill Haywood's comment.

What does it all mean? Clara Barnes caught my attention again; it was obvious that she could catch no one else's.

It means what you are willing or able to put into it, nothing more, I affirmed.

Well, said Clara, yawning, I guess I can't put much into it. This is worse than a party I went to last week, given by a baritone of the Aborn Opera Company.

At this point, a little school-marm type of person, with a sharp nose and eye-glasses, rose and shrilly began to complain.

I am a mere lay woman. I don't know a thing about modern art. I've been trying to learn something for five years. In the effort, I have attended all the meetings of this kind that I could in Paris, New York, and London. There's always a lot of talk but nothing is ever clear. Now I'd like to know if there isn't some explanation of modern art, an explanation that a mere lay woman could understand.

There was a ripple of amused laughter among the young artists and a rapid exchange of glances, but not one of them rose. Instead, a rather massive female, utterly unknown to me, with as many rows of gold braid across her chest as a French academician, a porter at the Crédit Lyonnais, or a soldier in the army of the Prince of Monaco, stood on her feet.

What, exactly, would you like to know? she asked in a voice in which authority and confidence were equal elements.

I'd like to know everything, but I'd be satisfied with anything. What, for instance, is the meaning of that picture?

She pointed to Andrew Dasburg's The Absence of Edith Dale, a cubistic contribution to æsthetic production in several planes and the colours of red, yellow, and blue.

The massive lady began with some hesitation. Her confidence had not deserted her but she seemed to be searching for precise words.

Well, she said, that picture is the kind of picture that gives pleasure to the kind of people who like that kind of picture. The arrangement of planes and colours is very satisfying. Perhaps I could explain it to you in terms of music. Do you understand the terminology of music?

Not at all, snapped the little woman with the eye-glasses.

The massive lady seemed gratified and continued, In that case, you may have difficulty in following me, but if you take the first and second themes of a sonata, their statement, the development or working-out section, the recapitulation, the coda. . . It has some relation to the sonata form certainly, but. . . The artist is in the room, the artist who painted the picture. Won't you explain the picture, Mr. Dasburg?

Andrew, very much amused, did not take the trouble to rise.

The picture is there, he said. You can look at it. Then, after a pause, he added, Henry James says, Woe, in the æsthetic line, to any example that requires the escort of precept. It is like a guest arriving to dine accompanied by constables.

Then, said the little lady, solemnly, I say, Woe to that picture, woe to it, for it certainly requires the escort of precept. Moreover, I don't think any one here knows anything, not a thing! she cried, her voice rising to a shrill intensity, not a blessed thing. It's just like the last chapter of Alice. If I shouted, Why, you're only a pack of cards, you'd all fly up in the air, a lot of flat paste-boards with kings, queens, aces, and deuces painted on your faces! I shall never ask another question about modern art. My private impression is that it's just so much junk.

Very indignant now, she wrapped an ice-wool shawl around her bony shoulders and made her way out of the room.

There wasn't an instant's pause and her departure caused no comment. A new speaker began,

The world, it may be stated, for the purposes of classification, is divided into four groups: the proletariat, the aristocrats, the middle class, and the artist class. The artist class may be called by any other name, bohemians, anarchists, revolutionists, what you will. It includes those who think and act freely, without traditions or inhibitions, and not all people who write or paint belong to this class at all. The artist class lives the way it *wants* to live. The proletariat and the aristocrats live the way they *have* to live. The middle class is composed of members of the proletariat trying to live like the aristocrats. . .

My mind wandered. I glanced across at Peter. He was still absorbed in Mahalah Wiggins and did not appear to be listening to the speaker. Yet, if he were really writing a realistic novel, the talk, the whole atmosphere of the evening should have interested and enthralled him. He never looked up and he was whispering very rapidly.

Some people resemble animals; some, perhaps, minerals; assuredly, some resemble flowers. Mahalah Wiggins was like a pansy. Her hair was black with purple lights; her eyes were a pale pansy blue; her face bore an ingenuous pansy expression that made one wonder why pansies were for thoughts. She wore a purple velvet dress with long tight sleeves ending in points which reached her knuckles, and, around her throat, a chain of crystal beads that hung almost to her waist.

Intercepting the long look I gave the girl, Neith Boyce smiled.

Are you, too, interested in Mahalah? she asked.

I am interested in the effect she is making.

She always makes an effect, Neith rejoined.

Who is she?

An orphan. Her father left her a little money, which she is spending at the Art Students' League, trying to learn to draw. Her only real talents are obvious. She knows how to dress herself and she knows how to attract men. Your friend seems to like her.

He does, indeed.

Mahalah comes here often and always spends the evening in a corner with some man. She seems to prefer married men. Is your friend married?

No.

A fat woman in a grey crêpe dress, embroidered in steel beads, standing in the centre of the room, shifted my attention.

Who is that? I asked.

That is *Miss* Gladys Waine, replied Neith. She is the wife of Horace Arlington, the sculptor.

Miss and a wife? What is she then, herself?

Nothing. She does not write, or paint, or compose. She isn't an actress. She is nothing but a wife, but she insists on retaining her individuality and her name. If any one addresses her as Mrs. Arlington, she is furious, and if you telephone her house and ask for Mrs. Arlington, although she may answer the telephone herself, she will assure you that Mrs. Arlington is not in, does not, in fact, live there at all. She adores Horace, too. The curious thing is that Horace's first wife, who divorced him, has never given up his name, of which she appears to be very proud. She is always called Mrs. Horace Arlington and trembles with rage when some tactless person remembers her own name.

My anonymous companion was by my side again with a plate of chocolate ice cream which he offered me.

Did you ever try eating chocolate ice cream and smoking a cigarette simultaneously? he asked. If you haven't, allow me to recommend the combination. The flavour of both cigarette and ice cream is immensely improved.

An old lady with an ear-trumpet, thinking she had been addressed, took the plate of ice cream from his outstretched hand, leaned over us and queried, Eh?

I say, said my incognito companion, that there is nothing like a good dose of castor oil.

Nothing like it for what? she shrieked.

As a carminative! he yelled.

But I don't suffer from that complaint, she argued.

Allow me to congratulate you, madame, and he bowed to her.

As we were saying, he continued, in a confidential manner, grasping my arm, one cannot be too careful in writing a drama. Weak, low-born people in trouble are pathetic; the middle classes in the same plight are subjects for melodrama or comedy; but tragedy should deal with kings and queens.

The groups separated, came together, separated, came together, separated, came together: syndicalists, capitalists, revolutionists, anarchists, artists, writers, actresses, "perfumed with botanical creams," feminists, and malthusians were all mixed in this strange salad. I talked with one and then another, smoking constantly and drinking a great deal of Scotch whisky. Somehow, my strange companion, like the Duchess in Alice, contrived always to be at my side. Remembering the situation at the Queen's croquet party, I could not help feeling grateful that his chin was square and that he was shorter than I. At one o'clock I had a headache and decided to go home. I looked for Edith.

She went to bed hours ago, Neith explained.

Then I made a vain search through the rooms for Peter.

One of the two young men who had dined with us stopped me.

If you are searching for your friend, he said, he went away with Mahalah Wiggins.

VIII

Friendship usually creates onerous obligations. Our friends are inclined to become exigent and demanding. They learn to expect attentions from us and are hurt when we do not live up to these expectations. Friends have an unpleasant habit of weighing on our consciences, occupying too much of our time, and chiding us because we have failed them in some unimportant particular. Is it strange that there are moments when we hate them? Friendship, indeed, is as perilous a relationship as marriage; it, too, entails responsibility, that great god whose existence burdens our lives. Seemingly we never escape from his influence. Each newly contracted friendship brings another sacrifice to the altar of this very Christian divinity. But there was no responsibility connected with my friendship for Peter. That is why I liked him so much. When he went away, he seldom notified me of his departure; he never wrote letters, and, when he returned, I usually re-encountered him by accident. In the whole of our long acquaintance, there never was a period in which he expected me to telephone him after a decent interval. We were both free in our relationship, as free as it is possible for two people, who are fond of each other, to be. There was a great charm in this.

A whole month went by, after Edith Dale's party, without my hearing from him. Then I sought him out. By this time, I knew him well enough to be prepared for some transmutation; but I was scarcely prepared for what I saw. His room on East Broadway had been painted ivory-white. On the walls hung three or four pictures, one of Marsden Hartley's mountain series, a Chinese juggler in water colour by Charles Demuth, a Picabia, which ostensibly represented the mechanism of a locomotive, with real convex brass piston-rods protruding from the canvas, a chocolate grinder by Marcel Duchamp, and an early Picasso, depicting a very sick-looking pale green woman, lying naked in the gutter of a dank green street. There were lovely desks and tables, Adam and Louis XIV and François I, a chaise longue, banked with striated taffeta cushions, purple bowls filled with spiked, blue flowers, Bergamo and Oushak rugs, and books bound in gay Florentine wall-papers. The bed was covered with a Hungarian homespun linen spread, embroidered in gay worsteds. The sun poured through the window over George Moore's ample back and he looked happier.

Peter was wearing green trousers, a white silk shirt, a tie of Chinese blue brocade, clasped with a black opal, and a most ornate black Chinese dressing-gown, around the skirt of which a silver dragon chased his tail. He was combed and brushed and there was a faint odour of toilet-water. His nails were manicured and on one of his little fingers I observed a ring which I had never seen him wear before. Later, when I examined it more closely, it proved to be an amethyst intaglio, with Leda and the Swan for its subject. It has been said, perhaps too often, that you cannot make a silk purse out of a sow's ear. It is even more true that you cannot make a sow's ear out of a silk purse.

I rose to the room: It's nicer than Edith's.

It's not bad, Peter admitted. I didn't get it fixed up at first. I like it better now, don't you?

I liked your friend, the other night, he continued.

You mean Edith?

Yes, you must take me there again.

I'm sorry but that is impossible. She has given up her apartment and returned to Florence. But, I added, I didn't know that you had talked together.

We didn't exchange three words, not even two, he said, but I took her in and she took me in. We like each other, I'm sure, and some day we'll meet again. Look, he added, sweeping his arm around, see what her glamour has given me, a new life!

But why did you leave so early?

I met a girl. . .

The next few weeks have left a rather confused impression in my mind, perhaps because Peter himself seemed to be confused. He never spoke of his book. Occasionally we went to the theatre or to a concert. I remember a concert of Negro music at Carnegie Hall, when there were twenty-four pianos and thirty banjos in the band and the Negroes sang G'wine up, Go Down, Moses, Rise and Shine, Run Mary, Run, and Swing Low, Sweet Chariot, with less of the old plantation spirit than either Peter or I could have assumed, but when the band broke into ragtime, the banjos twanged, the pianos banged, the blacks swayed back and forth, the roof was raised, and glory was upon us. Once, coming out of Æolian Hall, after a concert given by Elena Gerhardt, we were confronted by a wagon-load of double basses in their trunks. Two of the monsters, with their fat bellies and their long necks, stood vis-à-vis on the sidewalk and seemed to be conversing, while their brothers on the wagon, a full nine, wore the most ridiculously dégagé air of dignity. We will not sit down, not here at any rate, they plainly said, but they did not complain. Peter laughed a good deal at them and remarked that the aristocrats in the French Revolution must have gone to the guillotine in much the same manner, only the absurd double basses in their trunks had no roses to smell. Never have I seen inanimate objects so animate save once, at a rehearsal in the darkened Belasco Theatre, when the curly gold backs of the ornate chairs, peeping over the rails of the boxes, assumed the exact appearance of Louis XIV wigs on stately gentlemen. We heard Toscanini conduct the Ninth Symphony at the Metropolitan Opera House and we went to see Mrs. Leslie Carter play Paula Tanqueray. Often, in those days, we dined at the Pavillon d'Orient, an Armenian restaurant on Lexington Avenue. Peter particularly enjoyed a pudding called Tavouk Gheoksu, made of shredded chicken-breasts, pounded rice flour, powdered sugar, and cinnamon, and Midia Dolma, which are mussels stuffed with raisins and rice and pignolia nuts. Studying the menu one night, it occurred to him. that the names of the dishes would make excellent names for the characters of a play. The heroine, of course, he said, would be Lahana Sarma and the adventuress, Sgara Keofté; Enguinar is a splendid name for a hero, and the villain should be called Ajem Pilaf! There was a negro café in the basement of a building on Thirty-eighth street, which we frequently visited to see a most amazing mulatto girl, apparently boneless, fling herself about while a pitch-black boy with ivory teeth pummelled his drum, at intervals tossing his sticks high in the air and catching them dexterously, and the pianist pounded Will Tyers's Maori out of the piano. Occasionally we patronized more conventional cafés, one especially, where Peter was interested in a dancer, who painted her face with Armenian bole and said she was a descendant of a Hindu Rajah.

It was during this period that Peter nourished a desire to be tattooed and we sought out masters of the art on the Bowery and at Coney Island. For hours at a time he would examine the albums of designs or watch the artist at work decorating sailors and stevedores. One of these young men came nearly every day until his entire body, with the exception of his eye-balls, lips, and nails, had become a living Persian carpet, a subtle tracery of arabesques and fantastic beasts, birds and reptiles. The process of application was interesting. First, the pattern must be pricked out on glazed paper, smeared with lamp-black; this was laid on the surface to be tattooed and the outline left by the lamp-black was worked over with needles. The artist utilized a piece of wood into which were fixed with wires, nine or ten sharp points. The victims seemed to suffer a good deal of pain, but they suffered in silence. It was not, however, fear of pain that caused Peter to hesitate. I think he would have been frescoed from head to foot, could he have once decided upon a design. Day after day, he looked over the sketches, professional symbols, military, patriotic, and religious, symbols of love, metaphorical emblems and emblems fantastic and historical, frogs, tarantulas, serpents, hearts transfixed with arrows, crosses surmounted by spheres, and cannon. He was most tempted, I think, by the design of an Indian holding aloft the flag of the United States.

Late in March, he suggested a trip to Bermuda.

We must go somewhere, he explained, and why not Bermuda? It's not too far away.

I had been working hard and welcomed the idea of a vacation. To the question of a destination I was comparatively indifferent. It was, however, not too easy to arrange for even a brief leave of absence from the Times during the busy Winter months. By pleading incipient nervous prostration, however, I managed to accomplish my purpose.

On the day marked for our departure, I set out, bags in hands, for the office of the steamship company on lower Broadway, where Peter had commissioned me to stop for the tickets. There, a clerk behind the counter gave me a note. It was from Peter.

Dear Carl, it ran, I've cancelled our bookings. I can't go. Come in to see me today and we'll arrange another trip.

An hour later I found Peter in bed in his room on East Broadway. He was consuming a raw-beef sandwich but he laid it down to grasp my hand.

I'm sorry, he began, but I don't know how I ever happened to hit on the idea of Bermuda. When I awoke this morning, the thought appalled me; I couldn't get out of bed.

The counterpane was strewn with pamphlets relating to foreign travel. The telephone rang.

Excuse me, he said, as he clutched the receiver. Then, by way of explanation, It's the agent of the Cunard Line. I want to ask about the southern route.

He did. He asked about sailings for Italy, Africa, India, and even Liverpool and then he told the agent that he could not decide what to do but he would let him know later.

Carl, he exclaimed suddenly, let's go to Alaska!

I shook my head.

It may be that we shall meet there by chance some day, but I don't believe you can make up your mind to go there this week.

I'm afraid not, he assented ruefully. I suppose it's hard for you to understand.

I understand well enough, I replied, but under the circumstances you will have to travel alone or get some one else to go with you. While you are deciding, my leave of absence will expire.

A few days later he telephoned me.

I'm really going to Bermuda, was his message. I've had bookings on every boat sailing for Europe the past week and cancelled them all. My first idea was the right one. Bermuda is a change, it's near at hand, and I can get back quickly if I don't like it. Come to Bermuda with me, Carl!

When are you sailing? I asked. I'll come down to see you off.

On the day set, I went to the wharf, and to my great surprise, found Peter there, just as he had promised he would be, an hour before sailing time. If he kept an engagement at all, he always kept it on time. He had made preparations, buying new summer clothes, he explained, and a new innovation trunk. As he never knew how long he would stay in one place or where he would go from there, he always carried a great deal of apparently unnecessary baggage. This time he had five trunks with him and several bags, including two for the cats. As we stood on the wharf together, we saw these trunks being hoisted aboard. Then we walked up the gang-plank and went to seek out his cabin. He did not like it, of course, and he hunted up the purser and asked to be transferred to another part of the boat. The ship was crowded and no other cabin was vacant, but the purser, spurred to extra effort by the tip which Peter handed him, promised to try to get him one of the officers' rooms. A little later this transfer was effected and, before I left the boat, Peter was installed in his new quarters. As I bade him farewell, I thought he looked a little wistful. I watched the boat pull out into the river.

Five hours later, as I was working in the tower of the New York Times, I was called to the telephone.

I said, Hello, and almost dropped the receiver, for I had heard Peter's voice from the other end of the wire.

I'm back on East Broadway, he groaned. Do come down.

When I arrived, I found him propped up in bed, drinking tea, which he shared with me.

I just couldn't go! It wouldn't have been right to go feeling the way I did about it. Something dreadful would have happened.

But I saw the boat cast off her moorings.

Peter grinned.

We were steaming down the river. I was very tired and, having the desire to rest in bed, I began to undress. Suddenly it came over me that I had made a great mistake. I put my clothes on again rapidly, dashed to the deck, and hunted up the purser. You know, he had already befriended me. I told him that I had just opened my mail and my telegrams and had run across one informing me of the violent illness of my father—you know how much that would really worry me!—and that I *must* go back. He informed me that this was impossible, but another bill—a very large one this time—made him more sympathetic and my disembarkation was arranged with the aid of a tug-boat. I even got my trunks off, but I had to cry a good deal to do that. I'm very sorry for you, Mr. Whiffle, the purser said. He will never forget me, I'm sure.

The telephone rang. Peter lifted the receiver from the hook and I heard him say, Please reserve me a deck cabin on the Kronprinz Wilhelm sailing tomorrow. He turned, as he put the receiver back: I'm not crazy about the North German Lloyd but I've already sailed this week on the French Line, the Holland-American, the Cunard, and the White Star. I had to change.

By telephone the next day, I learned that Peter had *not* sailed on the Kronprinz Wilhelm.

Do you know, he said, I've hit on a solution. I could not decide where to go—every place has its faults—but it has occurred to me that I am not compelled to go anywhere; I can stay on right here!

There is still a pendant to this part of my tale. In May, Peter informed me that he had rented a house on Long Island, a small cottage near Great Neck, with a big fire-place and furniture that would do. He took me out with him the first night. He had engaged a man and his wife, Negroes, to care for the place and cook. We enjoyed a very good dinner and he seemed to have settled down for the summer but in the morning, at breakfast, I, and the Negroes, learned that he was dissatisfied.

I don't like the place much, he explained, at least, I don't think I do. At least, I'm not going to stay here.

He paid the servants two weeks wages and dismissed them. Then he telephoned an expressman to call for his trunks, none of which had been opened. Carrying the bags, two of which contained cats, we caught the 9 o'clock train back to town.

Before this last fluctuation, some time in April, I think it was, Peter's father really did die. Peter did not go to Toledo for the funeral but, after it was over, Mrs. Whiffle came to New York and I met her one day at tea. There was no change in Peter; certainly not a band of black on his arm.

He did seem to have one fixed idea that spring, an idea that centred on marriage.

I'm not particularly in love with any one, he admitted, and so it is rather difficult to choose, but I want children and my children must have a mother. There is Mahalah Wiggins. . . and there is the Rajah's grand-daughter. Well, I don't know that they will marry me, but I must decide what I am going to do before I give them a chance to decide what they are going to do!

A week or so later: I've been considering this question of marriage. It's a serious step. I can't rush into a thing like that. Mahalah doesn't like cats. You know, I couldn't give up my cats. I can't marry a woman who doesn't like cats. Luckily I haven't asked her.

A few days later: I will marry Mahalah, I think. She understands me; she doesn't seem to mind the crazy things I do. She is beginning to like the cats. She is healthy and she might produce fine children.

Another interval and then: She has accepted me. Isn't it wonderful for her to love me at my age for my money alone!

The preparations for the wedding were portentous, although it was to be celebrated as quietly as possible. There were clothes to buy and an apartment to be furnished. He left the decision of the day and place to Mahalah—fortunately that was her affair—but there was endless discussion about the honeymoon. He considered in turn nearly every spot on the globe, including Patagonia and Abyssinia. As the day in May set for the ceremony approached, Maine was mentioned rather more frequently than any other locality, but I had no real conviction that they would ultimately go there. I was to be the sole attendant at the wedding. That much seemed to be settled.

The great day dawned and brought with it a windy rain. I knew that Peter detested windy days; one of his superstitions associated them with disaster. He did not telephone me in the morning and his silence seemed ominous. Nevertheless, I put on a morning coat and a silk hat and presented myself at his rooms an hour before the minute set for the ceremony, which was to be celebrated in a little church in the neighbourhood. On another day, I would not have been surprised to find a note from Peter instead of himself but when, on reaching the top landing, I discovered the door open, and an old charwoman, packing up books and bowls inside, handed me a note with the superfluous information that Mr. Whiffle had gone away, my knees shook to such an extent that I wondered if I had suddenly become afflicted with tabes.

I managed to ask, Where?

I dunno, sir. He took his trunks.

I opened the letter.

Dear Carl, it ran, I just couldn't do it. It wouldn't be right to do it, if I feel that way, would it? And I do, indeed, I do! I told you I was not in love and it's hard to make up your mind if you don't feel strongly enough, and I never feel strongly enough about anything until afterwards. You know that. Now, that's soon enough about Bermuda or a house in the country, but it's too late in marriage. So I've just called it off. I've written her a note which doesn't exactly explain anything but some day she'll be glad, I hope, and so all *you* have to do is to make her feel that it's all right. Somehow, I believe she will understand. Anyway, I don't think she will be surprised. I'm going to Africa and, if I ever have an address again, I'll send it to you.

Peter

IX

In September, 1913, I found myself on the Paris-Milan Express on my way to Venice to meet Edith Dale. I have travelled across Switzerland many times and I hope to do so again (the view from the car windows is magnificent), but I shall never visit that country. God keep me from lingering in the mountains or by the shores of the sea. Such immensities of nature strangle talent and even dwarf genius. No great creative work has ever been composed by the sea or in the shadow of a mountain. In the presence of the perpetual mysteries of nature, man feels his smallness. There are those who may say that the sky-scrapers of the city evoke a similar feeling, but man's relation to these is not the same; he knows that man built these monster structures and that man will tear them down again. Mountains and the sea are eternal. Does this explain why so much that passes for art in America comes from Indiana and Illinois, the flat, unimposing, monotonous Middle West?

All journeys, I suppose, have their memorable incidents and episodes, however unimportant. My sole memory of this particular hegira is trifling. While I was dining, the train gave a lurch or a swerve, hurling me with my plate in my lap to the farthest corner of the car. The soup which the plate contained was in my lap, too, and elsewhere. Fortunately, the soup was not too hot. The accident recalled how once in a French drawing-room I had spilled a cup of calid coffee on my leg, scorching it painfully. The hostess was concerned about her carpet. I do hope, she was saying, that you haven't spilled your coffee on my carpet. I had not, but my leg was burned so badly and I felt so outraged by her lack of sympathy, that I took occasion later to make good the omission. Another night, another year, and certainly another place, a celebrated lady, next to whom I was sitting at supper, whisperingly adjured me to upset my coffee into her lap. She was wearing a new and elaborate frock and, astonished by her unreasonable request, I was dilatory in obeying. She whispered again, this time more sharply, Do as I tell you! At last I obeyed her, but the attempt at carelessness must have seemed very clumsy. I am a poor actor. Apologize, was her next command. Meekly, I followed instructions. Now she spoke aloud. It doesn't matter at all, she said. It's only an old rag. The other gentlemen present condoled with her, but she smilingly put them off, Don't make the boy feel bad. It wasn't his fault. Next day, while I lunched with her, a great many boxes arrived from Bendel's and Hickson's. Every man who had attended the supper had bought her a new dress, as she had been sure they would!

Towards nightfall, we approached the Italian border and after we had passed into Italy, the compartment, which had been crowded all day, was empty but for me and another man. As he was a Roumanian, who spoke neither French nor English, we did not converse. About 8 o'clock, we lay down on our respective seats and tried to sleep. It was nearly midnight when we arrived at Milan and I was glad to descend from the train, after the long journey, to take a few hours repose at a hotel near the station. Early in the morning, which was bright and sunny, I departed for Venice.

In the evening of that day, I was sitting at a table in the garden of Bonvecchiati's with Edith, who had motored down from Florence. Since the night I had taken Peter to her house in Washington Square, I had seen her only for fleeting moments, but she bridged the months immediately. Peter had been correct in his assumption that she would remember him. In fact, one of the first questions she asked was:

Where is that boy you brought to my house the other night?

It was "the other night" to Edith; months and even years meant nothing to her.

Peter Whiffle?

Yes, a nice boy. I liked him. Where is he? Let's take him back to Florence with us.

I don't know where he is.

Then I told her the story of how Peter did not get married.

I knew he was amusing. Let's get in touch with his vibrations and find him.

Edith, indeed, had invented her own kind of wireless long before Marconi came along with his. Distances, as a matter of fact, circumscribed her even less than time.

Just then, she saw Constant Lounsberry, or some one else, at a table in the corner of the garden where we were dining and she strolled over to talk with her. Sipping my coffee and smoking my cigarette, I recognized a familiar voice and turned to see Peter, with his mother, about to claim an adjacent table from which the occupants were rising. He looked two years younger than he had four months before and his rather pretty mother helped to confirm the illusion. Of course, I joined them at once and soon we were discussing the Italian futurists, the comparative merits of spaghetti and risotto, Lydia Borelli, the moving pictures, and the Marchesa Casati, who had given a magnificent festa the evening previous, when, clad in a leopard's pelt, she had stood on the steps of her palace, and greeted her guests as they approached by gondola on the Canale Grande. Peter, I noted, was wearing his amethyst intaglio of Leda and the Swan on the little finger of his left hand. After a time, during which, for a brief few moments, the conversation drifted towards Toledo and the small affairs of Mrs. Whiffle, he told me his story.

I came near dying in Africa, Carl, surrounded by niggers and fleas! It was horrible. Hot as a New York roof-garden and nearly as uncomfortable. There I lay, rotting with a nameless fever, no one with me but an incompetent Dutch doctor, who was more ignorant of the nature of my complaint than I was myself, and a half-naked aboriginal, who wanted to call in the witch-doctor and who, when burked in this direction, attempted a few amateur charms, which at least had the merit of awakening my interest. There I lay in a rude thatched hut with a roof of caked cow-dung; I couldn't eat, drink, or speak. I thought it was the end. Funny, but the only sound that reached my ears, after a few days, was the chattering of monkeys, and later they told me there were no monkeys about at all.

Over my head on the wall, hung a dirty thonged whip. Whether its purpose was to beat women or oxen, I don't know, but, you will remember, perhaps, that sometimes, when I awaken from sleep in the middle of the night, I have a strange habit of holding one arm straight up in the air, at right angles with my body. Well, while I was ill, there it was, most of the time, straight up! One night, when my strength was fast ebbing away, I reached higher and grasped the whip. Then I grew drowsy; everything seemed to turn blood-red, even the palm-leaves that waved across the opening made by the doorway of the hut, and it was very hot, unspeakably roasting. Now, through this same doorway, walked a woman in a rusty black robe and, although I knew it must be Death, the figure confused itself in my mind with Kathleen-ni-Houlihan and (will you believe it?) Sara Allgood! Fancy the appearance of Death in the middle of Africa suggesting to me the character of an Irish play and the actress I had seen in it! There followed a slight pause, during which Death stood perfectly still. Then two more figures entered the tiny hut. One was the Devil, Ahriman, Abaddon, what you will; I recognized him at once, he was so likable and, besides, he was lame. The other, I gathered after a little conversation, was an emissary from heaven. Eblis seated himself on one side of my cot, resting his crutches against the wall, and Gabriel's ambassador stood on the other side. Now these two droll fellows began to describe the climates and amusements of heaven and hell to me, each speaking in his turn, and continually interrupting themselves to beg me to decide speedily where I wanted to go. They stated frankly that they had not any too much time, as they had several other visits to make before dinner in various parts of the world. The Angel polished his feathers with a small hat-brush and the Devil seemed to be taking good care of his nails, in default of the opportunity to visit a manicure. Death stood immovable, inexorable. Imagine, even in her presence, I had to make up my mind where I wanted to go. It was a terrible experience, I can tell you! It was as if she were saying, Hurry now, hurry now! Nine minutes more. Only, of course, she did not utter a single word. The Angel and the Devil were too silly. Had they been silent, it would have been so much easier for me to decide. My mind would just be wavering in a certain direction, when one of the supernatural visitors would put me completely out with a warning about his rival's domain and a word of enthusiasm for his own. Never have I suffered such agony. I could not decide whether to go to Paradise or Pandemonium. My perplexity grew as they argued. Meantime, it was obvious that I was keeping Death from other bedsides. I could see that she was becoming nervous and irritable, shifting first on one foot, then on the other. It was evidently very irksome to her that she had taken a vow of silence. In life, it is so easy; there is always something else to do. But, in death, Carl, there is a single alternative; at least, it seemed so to me for an unconscionable space of time. Suddenly, however, two ideas occurred to me: I remembered that I had read somewhere that demon and deity were originally derived from the same root: in that case, one place would be as bad or as good as the other; and I remembered my solution of the Bermuda problem: I could stay where I was. *I was not compelled to go anywhere.* Stretching up my hands, I pulled hard on the whip, which must have broken loose from the nail, because when I came out of my coma, the thongs were gripped tightly in my hand, lying on the blanket.

Peter concluded his story and, suddenly, with that delightful inconsequence, which contributed so definite a charm to his manner, he pointed to a woman in the crowd.

She resembles an ostrich and she is dressed like a peacock, he said.

Peter, I wish you wouldn't jest about death and holy things, interjected Mrs. Whiffle, on whose literal mind the tale had evidently clawed as an eagle claws the brain of a cat.

But, mother, Peter tried to mollify her, I am not jesting. I am telling you something that happened.

Something that you *thought* had happened, Mrs. Whiffle corrected, but we should only think good thoughts. We should keep the dark ones out of our minds, especially when they interfere and conflict with the powerful words of Almighty God, our Creator.

I'm sorry, mother, I won't tell it again, he said, simply. Then, after a nibble or two at a lobster, he turned to me, Mother is going to America tomorrow. I shall be alone. Have you been to the Austrian Tyrol? There's Russia, of course, and Spain, and those islands where Synge used to go. Where are they? And Bucharest. Carlo, will you go with me tomorrow to Buenos Ayres or Helsingfors?

You are not to be told where you are going, I replied, but you are going with me.

Experience has taught me that people with principles are invariably unreasonable. Peter had no principles and therefore he was reasonable. So the next day, he really did drive back with us to Florence, through, the pleasant olive groves and vineyards. A jeroboam of chianti enlivened the journey, and Edith adored the story of Peter's encounter with Death, the Devil, and the Angel.

The Villa Allegra is set on the hills of Arcetri, high above the long cypress-bordered avenue called the Stradone del Poggio Imperiale. The villa is so artfully concealed amongst the cunningly-grouped, gnarled olive trees, eucalypti, myrtles, plane-trees, laurels, pepper-trees, and rows of cypresses, that, until you are in the very courtyard, you are unaware of its propinquity, although, by some curious paradox, the view from the loggia commands the surrounding country. The lovely curve of the façade has been attributed to the hand of Raphael, and Brunelleschi is said to have designed the cortile, for the physician of the Medici once inhabited this country house, but the completely successful loggia and the great salone were added by Chester Dale.

Peter had never been in Florence before; no more had I; so the romantic charm of this lovely old house in the mountains served to occupy us for several days. We inspected the sunken Roman bath and were thrilled by the rope-ladder, which, when lowered through a trap-door, connected a chamber on the second storey with a room on the first. We were satisfied to sit in the evening under the red brocaded walls, illuminated by wax tapers set in girandoles of green and rose faience, to stroll in the gardens, to gaze off towards the distant hills from the loggia. Edith entertained us with long accounts of the visits of the spectre, the dame blanche who haunted the house. It was, if the servants who swore they had seen her were to be believed, the spirit of an elderly maiden lady who had died there. In life, it seems, she had been of a jealous disposition and had tried to make the villa uncomfortable for other guests. She was not successful in this effort until she died, and not altogether successful even then, for there were those who refused to be terrified by the persistent presence of this spinster eidolon, which manifested itself in various ways. Others, however, resembled Madame de Staël, who did not believe in ghosts but was afraid of them.

In the mornings, Peter and I breakfasted together in the garden, whither was borne us by the cynical butler a tray with individual coffee percolators, a plate of fresh rolls, and a bowl of honey. The peacocks strutted the terrace and the breeze blew the branches of the fragrant gardenias across our noses. In the distance, the bells of Florence softly tolled. In the afternoon, the distant hills became purple and, in the evening, the atmosphere was tinged with green. The peasants sang in the road below and the nightingales sang in the olive copse. Roman lamps flickered on the tables and Strega, the golden witch-liquid, stood in our tiny crumpled Venetian tumblers, their distorted little bellies flecked with specks of gold. There were occasional callers but no other resident guests than ourselves at the villa and Edith, as was her custom, left us a good deal alone. On the day of our arrival, indeed, she disappeared after luncheon and only returned two days later, when she explained that she had gone to visit a friend at Pisa. We usually met her at dinner when she came out to the garden-table, floating in white crêpe de chine, with a turban of turquoise blue or some vivid brilliant green, but during the day she was seldom visible. She ate her breakfast alone on the balcony above our bedroom, then read for an hour or two. What she did after, one never knew, save as she told of it.

Meanwhile, Peter and I wandered about, inspecting the shops on the Ponte Vecchio, tramping through the old palaces and galleries. Several times Peter paused; he hesitated for the longest time, I think, before the David of Donatello, that exquisite soft bronze of the Biblical lad, nude but for his wreathed helmet, standing in his adolescent slender beauty with one foot on the head of the decapitated giant. He carries a sword and over his face flutters a quizzical expression. Indeed, what

Walter Pater said of the face of Monna Lisa might equally well apply to the face of David. So remarked Peter, explaining that the quality of both the David and Leonardo's darling was the same, both possessed a compelling charm, and it was the charm of David which had slain the ugly giant, just as charm always kills ugliness. And he swore that this was the most beautiful object that the hand of man had yet created, an art expression which reached its emotional and intellectual zenith, and then he spoke of the advantage that sculpture enjoyed over painting.

One tires of a painting. It is always the same. There is never anything new in it. But with a statue, every different light gives it a novel value, *and it can be turned around*. When you tire of one aspect, you try another. That is why statues belong in houses and pictures belong in museums. You can visit the museum when you wish to look at a picture, but it is impossible to live with a picture, because it is always the same. You can kill any picture, even a picture by Velázquez, by hanging it on your own wall, for in a few days it becomes a commonplace to you, a habit, and at last one day you do not look at it any more, you scarcely are aware that it is there at all, and you are surprised when your friends speak of it, speak of it admiringly. Yes, you say, unconvinced, it is beautiful. But you do not believe it. On the other hand, a statue is new every day. Every passing cloud in the sky, every shifting of the location of a lamp, gives a new value to a statue, and when you tire of seeing it in the house, you can transfer it to the garden where it begins another avatar.

Leaving David behind us, we walked down the long, marble, fourteenth century stairway of the Palazzo del Podestà, into the magnificent court embellished with the armorial bearings of the old chief magistrates, out to the Via del Procónsolo, on through the winding streets to the Palazzo Riccardi, where Peter again paused before the frescoes of Benozzo Gozzoli. The Gifts of the Magi is the general title but Gozzoli, according to a pleasant custom of his epoch, has painted the Medici on a hunting expedition, the great Lorenzo on a white charger, with a spotted leopard at its heels, falcons on the wrists of his brilliant attendants, a long train of lovely boys, in purple and mulberry and blue and green and gold, the colours as fresh, perhaps, as the day they were painted. The most beautiful room in the world, Peter exclaimed, this little oratory about the size of a cubicle at Oxford, painted by candlelight, for until recently, there was no window in the room, and I believed him. I am not sure but, belike, I believe him still. Then Peter loved the walk in that gallery which connects the Pitti Palace with the

Uffizi, a long narrow gallery which runs over the shops of the Ponte Vecchio (was ever another bridge so richly endowed with artistic and commercial interest?), where hang the old portraits of the families who have reigned in Florence, and some others. Quaint old canvases, they are, by artists long forgotten and of people no longer remembered, but more interesting to Peter and me than the famous Botticellis and Bellinis and Giorgiones which crowded the walls of the galleries. As we stood before them, Peter imagined tales of adventure and romance to suit the subjects, pinning his narratives to the expression of a face, the style of a sleeve, the embroidery of a doublet, or to some accompanying puppet or pet, some ill-featured hunch-back dwarf.

Thus the days passed and Peter became dreamy and wistful and the charm of his spirit, I believe, was never before so poignant, for his chameleon soul had taken on the hue of the renaissance and its accompanying spirituality, the spirituality of the artist, the happy working artist contriving works of genius. He could have perfectly donned the costume of the cinquecento, for the revolutionary Peter of New York, the gay, faun-like Peter of Paris, had disappeared, and a Peter of reveries and dreams had usurped their place.

Never have I been so happy, he said to me on one of these days, as I am now. This is true beauty, the beauty of spirit, art which has nothing to do with life, which, indeed, makes you forget the existence of life. Of course, however, this is of no help to the contemporary artist. Confronted, on every hand, with perfection, he must lay down his chisel or his brush or his pen. Great art can never flourish here again. That is why Browning's poetry about Florence is so bad; why Ouida, perhaps a lesser artist, succeeded where Browning failed. This is the ideal spot in which to idle, to dream, even to think, but no work is possible here and that, perhaps, is why I love Florence so much. I feel that I could remain here always and, if I did I should do nothing, nothing, that is, but drink my coffee and eat my rolls and honey in the morning, gaze across to the hills and dream, stroll over the wondrous Ponte Santa Trinità, which connects us so gracefully with the Via Tornabuoni, wonder how Ghirlandaio achieved the naïve charm of the frescoes in the choir of Santa Maria Novella, nothing else but these things. And, of course, I should always avoid the Piazza Vittorio Emanuele.

But he had scarcely uttered the name before he determined that he must drink some beer and so we strolled across the Piazza, on which he had just placed a malison, into the Giubbe Rosse, full of Americans writing letters, and Swedes and Germans, reading their native papers. We sat down at a table just outside the door and asked one of the red-coats, whose scarlet jackets give this place its cant name, to bring us two steins of Münchener. Then came an anachronism, one of those anachronisms so unusual in Florence which, more than any other city, is all of a piece. A stage-coach, such a coach as one sees in old England, drawn by four horses, drove gaily through the square. The interior seemed empty but on the top sat several English girls in sprigged muslins, a few pale youths, and a hatless man with very long hair, who was clad in olive-green velvet.

Who is it? I asked a man at a neighbouring table.

And the reply came, That is Gordon Craig and his school.

A few days later, Peter encountered Papini, that strange and very ugly youth, who mingled his dreams and his politics, mixing mysticism and propaganda until one became uncertain whether he was seer or socialist, and Marinetti. He read Mafarka le Futuriste and Marinetti talked to him about war and vaudeville, noise and overthrow, excitement and destruction. Bomb the palaces and build factories where they stood! So Marinetti enjoined his followers. Whatever is today is art; whatever was yesterday is nothing, worse than nothing, refuse, manure. Peter was especially amused by Marinetti's war cry, Méprisez la femme! his banishment of the nude and adultery from art, which was to become entirely male. So, indeed, was life, for Marinetti exhorted his male disciples to bear their own children! All these ideas, Peter repeated to me in a dreamy, veiled voice, noting at the same time that one of Marinetti's arms was longer than the other. It did not seem quite the proper environment to carry on in this respect, but the words of the Italian futurist had indubitably made an impression. I could see that it was quite likely that Peter would become a Marinettist when he went back to New York.

At dinner, one night, it became apparent that Peter once more was considering his life work. One of the guests, a contessa with a florid face and an ample bosom, began to fulminate:

Art is magic. Art is a formula. Once master a formula and you can succeed in expressing yourself. Barrie has a formula. Shaw has a formula. Even George Cohan has a formula. Black magic, negromancy, that's what it is: the eye of a newt, the beak of a raven, herbs gathered at certain hours, the heart of a black cat, boiled in a pot together, call up the bright devils to do your bidding.

Art is a protest, corrected Mina Loy. Each artist is protesting against something: Hardy, against life itself; Shaw, against shams; Flaubert, against slipshod workmanship; George Moore, against prudery; Cunninghame Graham, against civilization; Arthur Machen, against reality; Theodore Dreiser, against style. . .

Never did I feel less sure of the meaning of art than I do here, surrounded by it, began Peter, although I have never been more conscious of it, more susceptible to real beauty, more lulled by its magic. Yet I do not understand its meaning. It does not help me to work out my own problems. The trails cross. For instance, here is Edith leading her own life; here are we all leading our own lives, as remote as possible from Donatello and Gozzoli. Here is Gordon Craig, dressed like Bunthorne, driving a stage-coach and sending out arcane but thundering manifestos against a theatre in which his mother and Eleanora Duse are such conspicuous examples; here is Papini working and dreaming; here is Marinetti shooting off fire-crackers; here are the Braggiottis, teaching young Americans the elements of music in that modern music-room with bas-relief portraits of the great composers, Beethoven, Bach, Verdi, Mozart, Wagner, Rossini. . . and Sebastian B. Schlesinger, moulded in the frieze. Here is Loeser, always building new houses and never completing them; here is Arthur Acton, with a chauffeur who sings tenor arias in the drawing-room after dinner; here is Leo Stein, collecting Renoirs and Cézannes for his villa at Settignano. What does it all mean, unless it means that everything should be scrambled together? I think a great book might be written if everything the hero thought and felt and observed could be put into it. You know how, in the old novel, only what is obviously essential to the plot or the development of character is selected. But a man, crossing a street to commit a murder, does not continuously think of the murder. The cry of Buns! hot cross buns! the smell of onions or dead fish, the sight of a pretty woman, impress his senses and remind him of still other things. These ideas, impressions, objects, should all be set down. Nothing should be omitted, nothing! One might write a whole book of two hundred thousand words about the events of an hour. And what a book! What a book!

This was before the day of Dorothy Richardson, James Joyce, and Marcel Proust. The contessa snorted. Mina Loy, at the other end of the table, looked interested in Peter for the first time, I thought. The white Persian cat, one of Edith's cats, with his superb porcelain-blue eyes, sauntered into the room, his tail raised proudly. Edith spoke:

The great artists put themselves into their work; the cat never does. Men like Stieglitz and de Meyer put themselves into their cameras, that is why their photographs are wonderful, but the cat never puts himself into a camera. The great conquerors put themselves into their actions; the cat never does. Lovers put themselves into the selves of their loved ones, seeking identity; the cat never does. Mystics try to lose themselves in union with their gods; the cat never does. Musicians put themselves into their instruments; the cat never does. Indian men, working in the ground, put themselves in the earth, in order to get themselves back in the forms of wheat or maize to nourish their bodies; the cat never does. Navajo women, when they weave blankets, go so completely into the blanket while they are working on it, that they always leave a path in the weaving that comes out at the last corner for their souls to get out of the blanket; otherwise they would be imprisoned in it. The cat never does things like this!

So every one really centres his self somewhere outside of himself; every one gets out of his body. The cat *never* does. Every one has a false centre. Only the cat—the feline—has a true centredness inside himself. Dogs and other animals centre themselves in people and are therefore open to influence. The cat stays at home inside his body and can never be influenced.

Every one has always worked magic through these false centres— doing things to himself—seeking outlets, seeking expression, seeking power, all of which are only temporarily satisfactory like a movement of the bowels, which is all it amounts to on the psychic plane. The cat *is* magic, *is* himself, *is* power. The cat knows how to live, staying as he does inside his own body, for that is the only place where he *can* live! That is the only place where he can experience being *here* and *now*.

Of course, all the false-centred people have a kind of magic power, for any centredness is power, but it doesn't last and it doesn't satisfy them. Art has been the greatest deceiver of all—the better the art, the greater the deception. It isn't necessary to objectify or express experience. What is necessary is to *be*. The cat knows this. May be, that is why the cat has been an object of worship; may be, the ancients felt intuitively that the cat had the truth in him.

Do you see where these reflections lead? The whole world is wildly pursuing a mirage; only the cat is at home, so to speak.

Actors understand this. They only get a sense of reality when they throw themselves into a part. . . a false centre.

The cat understands pure being, which is *all* we need to know and which it takes us a lifetime to learn. It is both subject and object. It is its own outlet and its own material. It *is*. All the rest of us are divided bits of self, some here, some there. The cat has a complete subjective unity. Being its own centre, it radiates electricity in all directions. It is magnetic and impervious. I have known people to keep a cat so that they could stroke the electricity out of it. Why didn't they know how to be electric as the cat *is*? The cat is the fine specimen of the I am. Who of us is so fully the I am that I am?

Look around the world! Everybody putting him*self out* in some form or another! Why? It doesn't do any good. At the end you exhaust the possibilities of the outside world—geographically and spiritually. You can use up the external. You can come to the end of objectifying and objectives, and then what? In the end, only what we started with—the Self in the body, the Self at home, where it was all the time while bits of it were wandering outside.

Peter applauded with sundry bravos and benisons and divers amens, but was moved to ask, Does the cat know this? Has the cat got a *conscious being?* Does he appreciate his advantage?

But no one answered these questions, least of all the haughty white Persian.

Apparently unreasonably (this biography was as far from my mind as anything well could be), following a habit which I never could explain to myself until I became a professional writer and the reason became clear, before going to bed, I made notes on this and several subsequent evenings and it is upon these notes that I am drawing now, to refresh my memory. A few nights later, when Edith and Peter and I were sitting alone on the loggia, Peter talked to us about the critics.

The trouble with the critics, he was saying, is that they are not contradictory enough. They stick to a theory for better or worse, as unwise men stick to an unwise marriage. Once they have exploited a postulate about art or about an artist, they make all his work conform to this postulate, if they admire it. On the other hand, if the work of an artist displeases them, they use the postulate as a hammer. I think it is Oscar Wilde who has written, Only mediocre minds are consistent. There is something very profound in this aphorism.

Consider Frank Harris's Shakespeare theory, for example. It is good enough as an idea, as a casual inspiration it is almost a masterpiece. It would make a fine essay; if it had been used as a passing reference in a book, it probably would have been quoted for years. Harris, however, has spun it out into two thick volumes and made it fit into crevices and crannies where it cannot very well feel at home. Certainly, it is true that any artist creates his characters out of his own virtues and weaknesses; all of a novelists' characters, to a certain extent, reflect phases of himself. The mistake Harris has made lies in identifying Shakespeare only with his weak, unsuccessful, sentimental, disappointed, unhappy characters, such as Hamlet, Macbeth, Orsino, Antonio, and Romeo. Shakespeare probably was just as much Sir Toby Belch and Falstaff. Curiously, this theory of identification fits the critic himself, the intellectual creator, more snugly than it does the romancer, the emotional creator. Remy de Gourmont has pointed this out. He says, Criticism is perhaps the most suggestive of literary forms; it is a perpetual confession; believing to analyze the works of others, the critic unveils and exposes himself to the public. So from these books we may learn more about Frank Harris than we do about Shakespeare.[1] This, of course, has its value.

But that is why Shakespeare is greater than his critics, that is greater than the critics who cling to one theory. Shakespeare speaks only through his characters and he can say, or make some one say,

Frailty, thy name is woman,

but on the next page another character may deny this sentiment, for this is not Shakespeare's opinion, it is that of an incensed lover. So Richard III remarks:

Conscience is but a word the cowards use,
Devised at first to keep the strong in awe.

But Hamlet replies:

Thus conscience does make cowards of us all.

Both are true, both good philosophy, and so from the playwright, the great poet, the novelist, you get a rounded view of life which a critic usually denies you.

---

1. In a later book, his biography of Oscar Wilde, Frank Harris tells us more about himself than he does about Wilde. C. V. V.

Occasionally a critic does contradict himself and really becomes human and delightful and we take him to our hearts, but the next day all the doctors and professors and pundits are excoriating him, assuring us that he is not consistent, that he is a loose writer, etc. Good critics, I should like to believe, are always loose writers; they perpetually contradict themselves; their work is invariably palinodal. How, otherwise, can they strive for vision, and how can they inspire vision in the reader without striving for vision themselves? Good critics should grope and, if they must define, they should constantly contradict their own definitions. In this way, in time, a certain understanding might be reached. For instance, how delightful of Anatole France to describe criticism as a soul's adventures among masterpieces, and then to devote his critical pen to minor poets and unimportant eighteenth century figures.

But, asked Edith, does not the reader in his own mind contradict the consistent critic? Does not this answer your purpose?

By no means. What you say is quite true. A dogmatic writer rouses a spirit of contradiction in the reader, but this is often a spirit of ire, of deep resentment. That is in itself, assuredly, something, but it is not the whole purpose of criticism to arouse anger, whatever the prima donna who reads the papers the morning after her début at the Opera may think. Criticism should open channels of thought and not close them; it should stimulate the soul and not revolt it. And criticism can only be wholesome and sane and spiritually stimulating when it is contradictory. I do not mean to say that a critic should never dogmatize—I suppose at this moment I myself appear to be dogmatizing! He may be as dogmatic as he pleases for a page or two pages, but it is unsafe to base an entire book on a single idea and it is still more unsafe to reflect this idea in one's next book. It is better to turn the leaf and begin afresh on a new page. Artists are never consistent. Ibsen apparently wrote A Doll's House to prove that the truth should always be told to one's nearest and dearest and, apparently, he wrote The Wild Duck to prove that it should not. Ibsen, you see, was a poet and he knew that both his theses were true. In his attempt to explain the revolutionary doctrines which he found inherent in Wagner's Ring, Bernard Shaw ran across many snags. He swam through the Rheingold, rode triumphantly through Die Walküre, even clambered gaily through Siegfried, by making the hero a protestant, but when he reached Götterdämmerung, his hobby-horse bucked and threw him. Shaw was forced to admit that Götterdämmerung was pure opera, and he attempted to evade the difficulty by explaining that Wagner wrote the book for this work before he wrote the other three, quite forgetting that, if Wagner's intention had been the creation of a revolutionary cycle, it would have been entirely possible for him to rewrite the last drama to fit the thesis. The fact is that the work is inconsistent from any point of view except the point of view of art. Any critic who is an artist will be equally inconsistent.

Truth! Truth! Peter cried in scorn. Forsooth, what is truth? Voltaire was right: error also has its merits.

And yet. . . I began.

And yet! he interrupted, still more scornfully. No, there is no such thing as truth. Truth is impossible. Truth is incredible. The most impossible and incredible physical, spiritual, or mental form or idea or conception in the cosmos is the cult of truth. Truth implies permanence and nothing is permanent. Truth implies omniscience and no one is omniscient. Truth implies community of feeling and no two human beings feel alike about anything, except perhaps for a few shifting seconds. Truth, well if there is such a thing as truth, we may at least say that it is beyond human power to recognize it.

But it is not impossible to approach Truth, to play around her, to almost catch her, to vision her, so to speak. No, that is not impossible. Natheless, the artist, the writer, the critic who most nearly approaches Truth is he who contradicts himself the oftenest and the loudest. One of the very best books James Huneker has written is a work purporting to come from the pen of a certain Old Fogy, in which that one opposes all of James's avowed opinions. It is probable, indeed, that we can get the clearest view of Huneker's ideas from this book.

Then truth is not an essential of art? I asked.

It has, of course, nothing whatever to do with art. No more has form. Life has so much form that art, which should never imitate life, should be utterly lacking in form. Criticism appears to be a case apart. Criticism is an attempt, at its worst at least, to define art and definition implies truth and error. But what the critics do not realize in their abortive efforts to capture her, is that Truth is elusive. She slips away if you try to pin her down. You must, as Matthew Arnold has said much better than I can, approach her from all sides. Even then she will elude you, for the reason I have elucidated, because she does not exist!

Why do we read the old critics? For ideas? Seldom. Style? More often. Anecdote? Always, when there is any. Spirit? We delight in it. Facts? Never. No, you will never find facts—at least about such a metaphysical concept as art—correctly stated in books, because there is no way of stating them correctly. And the evasion of facts is an exact science which has yet to become popular with the critics, although it is always popular with readers, as the continued success of Berlioz's Mémoires goes to show. We read the old critics *to find out about the critics*, not about the subjects on which they are writing. Consequently, it is only the critics who have been interesting personalities who are read through many generations.

As an addendum, I might state that interest in art is fatal. An enthusiastic essay will kill anything. Spontaneity and freshness do not withstand praise. Art must be devoid of self-consciousness. A certain famous actress once told me that she never liked to have people particularize in their enthusiasm about one of her performances. When, she said, they tell me that such and such a gesture, such and such a tone of voice, is the important moment in one of my interpretations, I can never repeat it without remembering their praise, and, involuntarily, something of the original freshness has departed.

I remember another occasion on which Peter talked about the subject that most interested him.

It is the pleasant custom of present day publishers of books, he was saying, to prelude the real publication of a volume by what is technically known as a dummy. The dummy, the sample from which orders are taken, to all outward inspection, appears to be precisely like the finished book. The covers, the labels, the painted top, and the uncut edges give one every reason to hope for a meaty interior. Once opened, however, the book offers the browser a succession of blank pages. Sheet after sheet of clean white paper slips through his fingers, unless, by some chance, he has opened the volume at the beginning, for the title-page and table of contents are printed (the dedication is missing), and so are the first thirteen pages of the text.

Such dummies are irresistible to me. Coming warm, hot even, from the binder, they palpitate with a suggestion which no perusal of their contents can disturb. How much better than the finished book! I exclaim, and there are days when I feel that I will never write a book; I will write only dummies. I would write a title-page, a table of contents, and thirteen pages of some ghost essay, breaking off in the middle of a curious phrase, leaving the reader sweetly bewildered in this maze of tender thought. And, to give this dummy over value, to heighten its charm and its mystery, I would add an index to the blank pages, wherein one could learn that on empty page 76 hovered the spirits of Heliogabalus and Gertrude Atherton. It would further inform one that Joe Jackson, George Augustus Sala, and fireless cookers were discussed on page 129. Fancy the reader's delight in learning that he might cull passages dealing with the breeding of white mice on unbegotten pages 67, 134, 185 et seq., 210, 347!

I have it in mind to call my first dummy, Shelling Peas for Shillings. The binding will be of magenta boards with a pistachio-green label, printed in magenta ink. The top will be stained pistachio-green and the edges will be unopened. On the title-page, I shall set an appropriate motto and a plausible table of contents might include:

The Incredible History of Ambrose Gwinett
Inkstains and Stoppage
Purcell, Polko, and Things Beginning with a P
Folk-Dancing at Coney Island
Carnegie Hall as a Cure for Insomnia
Many Blue Objects and One Black One
Ouida's Italy
Erasmus Darwin's Biographer
Etc.

You see how the subjects present images and ideas which will make it possible for the reader, in his mind's eye, to write the papers himself. Shelling Peas for Shillings, Peter rolled the name over. It's a good title. I shouldn't wonder if sometime that dummy would be much sought after by collectors.

X

My story rolls on. As I gaze back through the years, gathering the threads of this history together, trying to weave them into form, I am amazed to recall how very few times, comparatively speaking, Peter and I met. Yet, I suppose, I was his best friend during these years, at any rate his most sympathetic friend. If there were no other proof, his will would offer excellent evidence in this respect. But we saw each other seldom, for a few hours, a few days, at best for a few weeks, followed by a period of vacuum. I had my own interests and, doubtless, he had his. It was characteristic that he never wrote letters to me, with the exception of the one or two brief notes I have already inserted in the text. His personality, however, was so vivid, the impression he made on me was so deep, that he always seemed to be with me, even when the ocean separated us. As I write these lines, I could fancy that he stands beside me, a sombrely joyous spectre. I could believe that he bends over my shoulder or, at any rate, that presently I will hear a knock at the door and he will enter, as he entered Martha Baker's studio on that afternoon in May so long ago.

The magic Florentine days marched to a close. I say marched, but the musical form was more exactly that of a gavotte, a pavane, or a stately Polish dance, imagined by Frederic Chopin. It was too perfect to last, this life which appeared to assume the shape of conscious art. One afternoon, Peter and I motored to the old Villa Bombicci, the design of which legend has attributed to the hand of Michael Angelo. Now it had become a farmhouse, and pigs and chickens, a cock and a few hens, stray dogs and cats, wandered about in the carious cortile. We had come to bathe in the swimming-pool, a marble rectangle, guarded by a single column of what had once been the peristyle. A single column, a cornered wall, and a cluster of ivy: that was the picture. We could bathe nude, for the wall concealed the pool from the farmhouse.

Peter was the first to undress and, as he stood on the parapet of the pool by the broken column, his body glowing rose-ivory in the soft light of the setting sun, his head a mass of short black curls, he seemed a part of the scene, a strange visitor from the old faun-like epoch, and I could imagine a faint playing of pipes beyond the wall, and a row of Tanagra nymphs fleeing, terrified, in basso-rilievo. Sometime, somewhere, in the interval since the days when we had pursued the exterior decorators on the Bowery and at Coney Island, he had discovered an artist, for now his chest was tattooed with a fantastic bird of rose and blue, a bird of paradise, a sirgang, or, perhaps, a phœnix or a Zhar-Ptitsa, the beak pointing towards his throat, the feathers of the tail showering towards that portion of the body which is the centre of umbilicular contemplation among the Buddhists. He straightened his lithe body, lifted his arms, and dived into the pool, where he swam about like a dolphin. It was Peter's nature, as I must have made evident by now, to take the keenest joy in everything he did. Almost immediately, I followed and we puffed and blew, spattering the crystal drops about in the air, so that it seemed as if showers of stones fell sharply, stinging our faces, as we lay on our backs in the warm water. Eventually, clambering up to the parapet, we sat silent for many moments and I remember that a fleecy cloud passed over the face of the sinking sun. It was very still, save for the soft lowing of cattle in the distant mountains, the cackling of the hens in the courtyard, and the sweet tolling of faraway bells.

Peter broke the silence.

I am not going back to the villa, he said.

Peter! I exclaimed. But. . .

I didn't know until just now. I love the villa. I love Florence. I love Edith and I love you. I have never been so happy, but it couldn't last. Just now when we were spattering water I had a premonition. . . He laughed. There was once a singer—I do not recall her name, but it was neither Patti nor Jenny Lind—who retired while she was still in the best of voice, and those who heard her in her last opera will always remember what a great singer she was. So I am going away while I am happy, so that I can always remember that I have been perfectly happy—once.

But you always are. . .

There, you see, you think so! There are months and years when I am alone, when nobody sees me. Then I am struggling. I make a great deal of sport about work and, indeed, I *won't* work at anything that doesn't interest me, but you know, you *must* know by now, how much I want to write. It is coming so slowly. It is getting late. . . late. I must go away to think. I'm too happy here and I am losing time. He was very earnest now. I *must* write my book.

But you are coming back to the villa. Your clothes are there, and you will want to say good-bye to Edith.

No, that is just what I want to avoid and that is what you can do for me. I can't say good-bye to Edith. She would persuade me to stay. It would be so easy! You, especially, could persuade me to stay, but I know you won't, now that you understand how I feel. I shall catch the night express for Milan. Please, try to explain to Edith. . . and you can pack my bags and send them after me.

But where are you going?

I don't know, and even if I did know and told you, you might be certain that I would change my mind and go somewhere else. Dispatch my bags to the American Express Company in Paris and I will send for them.

When shall we meet again?

Peter stood up, his nude body outlined against the crumbling, pink, vine-covered wall. Then he turned and stooped to draw on his clothing.

Chi lo sa? It will be sometime. You are going back to New York?

Yes, very soon. Perhaps next week.

Well, if we don't meet somewhere else, I will go there to see you, that much I promise. Then, almost awkwardly, he added, I want you to have my ring. He drew off the amethyst intaglio of Leda and the Swan and handed it to me.

We dressed in silence. The motor stood waiting in the road beside the decrepit farmhouse, noble even in its decay. Peter asked the chauffeur to drive him to the station, before he should take me back to the Villa Allegra, and at the station we parted.

Dinner that night seemed tasteless. Edith was furious; I have seldom seen her so angry. It was exactly what she would have done herself, had she been so inclined, but she was not at all pleased to have Peter usurp her privileges. She hardly waited for the salad, leaving me to munch my cheese and drink my coffee alone. Following dinner, I sat, a solitary figure on the loggia, smoking a cigarette and sipping my Strega. Giuseppe, the boy who brought it to me, seemed as dispirited as the rest of us. After trying in vain to interest myself in half a dozen books, I went to bed and rolled about restlessly during the long hot night. I was up very early and went to the garden as usual, but now lonely and miserable, to have my breakfast. The butler, more cynical than ever, brought the tray. A gardenia and a note were added touches. They were Edith's farewells. She had departed for a motor trip through the Abruzzi. She might return in three weeks. I was welcome to stay at the villa and wait or. . . And so that summer ended.

A month later, Edith was back in New York and again I saw a good deal of her. She asked for news of Peter but I had none to give her. Other friends of mine who had heard about him from Edith, expressed a desire to meet him but, so far as I was concerned, I did not even know whether or not he was alive. In December, however, passing through Stuyvesant Square with its gaunt bare trees, the old red-brick Quaker school-houses, and the stately but ugly Saint George's, on my way to Second Avenue, where I intended to visit a shop where Hungarian music might be procured, I found him, sitting alone on a bench.

I am too happy to see you again, he greeted me, but only you. Edith must not be told that I am in New York, for at last I am working and I can afford no interruptions. Edith has a way of breaking up the rhythm of one's life and my life is very rhythmic just now. Do you remember, one night at the villa, there was some conversation about formulæ and black magic?

You mean the contessa. . .

She was speaking figuratively, perhaps, but I have taken her literally. He paused for a moment; then he continued, It is possible that you will also remember my telling you in Florence that I believed Donatello's David to be the most beautiful work of art in the world.

I remember; I still think you were right.

I haven't altered my opinion. It is the most beautiful *statue* I have ever seen, just as Debussy's l'Après-midi d'un Faune is the most beautiful music I have ever heard, just as The Hill of Dreams is—have you read it?

At that time, I had not, and I admitted it. I was even ignorant of the name of the author.

Now Peter, as he sat on the bench beside me, began to speak of Arthur Machen: The most wonderful man writing English today and nobody knows him! His material is handled with the most consummate art; arrangement, reserve, repose, the perfect word, are never lacking from his work and yet, at the age of fifty, he is an obscure reporter on a London newspaper. There are, of course, reasons for this neglect. It is a byword of the day that one only takes from a work of art what one brings to it, and how few readers can bring to Machen the requisite qualities; how few readers have gnosis!

Machen evokes beauty out of horror, mystery, and terror. He suggests the extremes of the terrible, the vicious, the most evil, by never describing them. His very reserve conveys the infinity of abomination.

You know how Algernon Blackwood documents his work and stops to explain his magic orgies, so that by the time you have finished reading one of his weird stories, you completely discount it. On the other hand, although Machen writes in the simplest English concerning the most unbelievable impieties, he never lifts the crimson curtain to permit you to see the sacrifice on the Manichean altar. He leaves that to the imagination. But his expression soars so high, there is such ecstasy in his prose, that we are not meanly thrilled or revolted by his negromancy; rather, we are uplifted and exalted by his suggestion of impurity and corruption, which leads us to ponder over the mysterious connection between man's religious and sensual natures. Think, for a moment, of the life of Paul Verlaine, dragged out with punks and pimps in the dirtiest holes of Paris, and compare it with the pure simplicity of his religious poetry. Think of the Song of Songs which is Solomon's and the ancient pagan erotic rites in the holy temples. Remember the Eros of the brothels and the Eros of the sacred mysteries. Recall the Rosicrucian significance of the phallus, and its cryptic perpetuation in the cross and the church steeple. In the middle ages, do not forget, the Madonna was both the Virgin Mother of Christ and the patron of thieves, strumpets, and murderers. Far surpassing all other conceivable worldly pleasures is the boon promised by the gratification of the sensual appetite; faith promises a bliss that will endure for ever. In either case the mind is conscious of the enormous importance of the object to be obtained. Machen achieves the soaring ecstasy of Keats's Ode on a Grecian Urn or Shelley's To a Skylark, and yet he seldom writes of cool, clean, beautiful things. Was ever a more malignantly depraved story written than The White People (which it might be profitable to compare with Henry James's The Turn of Screw), the story of a child who stumbles upon the performance of the horrid, supernatural rites of a forgotten race and the consequences of the discovery? Yet, Machen's genius burns so deep, his power is so wondrous, that the angels of Benozzo Gozzoli himself do not shine with more refulgent splendour than the outlines of this erotic tale, a tale which it would have been easy to vulgarize, which Blackwood, nay Poe himself, would have vulgarized, which Laforgue would have made grotesque or fantastic, which Baudelaire would have made poetic but obscene. But Machen's grace, his rare, ecstatic grace, is perpetual and unswerving. He creates his rhythmic circles without a break, the skies open to the reader, and the Lord, Jesus Christ, appears on a cloud, or Buddha sits placidly on his lotus. Even his name is mystic, for, according to the Arbatel of Magic, Machen is the name of the fourth heaven.

Machen does not often write of white magic; he is a negromancer; the baneful, the baleful, the horrendous are his subjects. With Baudelaire, he might pray, Evil be thou my good! Consider the theme of The Great God Pan, a psychic experiment, operation, if you will, on a pure young girl, and its consequences. Again a theme which another writer, any other writer, would have cheapened, filled in with sordid detail, described to the last black mass. But Machen knows better. He knows so much, indeed, that he is able to say nothing. He keeps the thaumaturgic secrets as the alchemists were bidden to do. Instead of raising the veil, he drops it. Instead of revealing, he conceals. The reader may imagine as much as he likes, or as much as he *can*, for nothing is said, but he rises from a reading of one of these books with a sense of exaltation, an awareness that he has tasted the waters of the Fountain of Beauty. There is, indeed, sometimes, in relation to this writer, a feeling[1] that he is truly inspired, that he is writing automatically of the eternal mysteries, that the hand which holds the pen is that of a blind genius, and yet. . .

More straightforward good English prose, limpid narrative, I am not yet acquainted with. What a teller of stories! This gift, tentatively displayed in The Chronicle of Clemendy, which purports to be a translation from an old manuscript—Machen has really been the translator of the Heptamaron, Béroalde de Verville's Moyen de Parvenir, and the Memoirs of Casanova—, flowered in The Three Imposters, nouvelles in the manner of the old Arabian authors. This work is not so well-known as The Dynamiter, which it somewhat resembles, but it deserves to be. Through it threads the theme, that of nearly all his tales, of the disintegration of a soul through an encounter with the mysteries which we are forbidden to know, the Sabbatic revels, the two-horned goat, alchemy, devil-worship, and the eternal and indescribable symbols. The problem is always the same, that of facing the great God Pan and the danger that lurks for the man who dares the facing.

And one wonders, Peter continued, his eyes dilating with an expression which may have been either intense curiosity or horror, one wonders what price Machen himself has paid to learn his secret of how

---

1. A feeling in which he encourages belief in his preface to a new edition of "The Great God Pan"; 1916.

to keep the secrets! He must have encountered this horror himself and yet he lives to ask the riddle in flowing prose! What has it cost him to learn the answer? Popularity? Perhaps, for he is an obscure reporter on a London newspaper and he drinks beer! That is all any Englishman I have asked can tell me about him. Nobody reads his books; nobody has read them. . . except the few who see and feel, and John Masefield is one of these. This master of English prose, this hierophant, who knows all the secrets and *keeps* them, this delver in forgotten lore, this wise poet who uplifts and inspires us, is an humble journalist and he drinks beer!

Peter paused and looked at me, possibly for corroboration, but what could I say? I had never, until then, touched upon Machen, although I remembered that Mina Loy had included him in her catalogue of protestants in the symposium at the Villa Allegra. Later, when I sought his books, I found them more difficult to arrive at than those of any of his contemporaries and today, thanks to the fame he has achieved through his invention of the mystic story of The Bowmen, the tale of the Angels at Mons, a story which was credited as true, for returning soldiers swore that they had really seen these angels who had led them into battle, thus arousing the inventive pride of the author, who published a preface to prove that the incident had never occurred except in his own brain, his early books command fantastic prices. Eight or nine pounds is asked for The Chronicle of Clemendy and forty or fifty pounds for his translation of Casanova. But on that day I said little about the matter, because I had nothing to say.

Now we were walking and presently stopped before Peter's door, a house on the south side of Stuyvesant Square, conveniently near, Peter observed, in sardonic reference to Marinetti's millennium, the Lying-in-Hospital. He unlocked the door and we entered. The hall was painted black and was entirely devoid of furniture. A lamp, depending on an iron chain from the ceiling, shed but a feeble glow, for it was enclosed in a globe of prelatial purple glass. We passed on to a chamber in which purple velvet curtains were caught back by heavy silver ropes, exposing at symmetrical intervals, the black walls, on which there were several pictures: Martin Schongauer's copperplate engraving of The Temptation of Saint Anthony, in which the most obscene and foulest of fiends tear and pull and bite the patient and kindly old man; Lucas Cranach's woodcut of the same subject, more fantastic but less terrifying; two or three of Goya's Caprichos; Félicien Rops's Le Vice Suprême, in which a skeleton in evening dress, holding his head in the curve of his elbow, chapeau claque in hand, opens wide an upright coffin to permit the emergence of a female skeleton in a fashionable robe; black ravens flit across the sky; Aubrey Beardsley's Messalina; Pieter Bruegel's allegorical copperplate of Lust, crammed with loathsome details; and William Blake's picture of Plague, in which a gigantic hideous form, pale-green, with the slime of stagnant pools, reeking with vegetable decays and gangrene, the face livid with the motley tints of pallor and putrescence, strides onward with extended arms, like a sower sowing his seeds, only the germs of his rancid harvest are not cast from his hands but drip from his fusty fingers. The carpet was black and in the very centre of the room was a huge silver table, fantastically carved, the top upheld by four basilisk caryatides. On this table stood a huge egg, round which was coiled a serpent, the whole fashioned from malachite, and a small cornelian casket, engraved in cuneiform characters. There were no windows in the room, and apparently no doors, for even the opening through which we had entered had disappeared, but the chamber was pleasantly lighted with a lambent glow, the origin of which it was impossible to discover, for no lamps were visible. In one corner, I noted a cabinet of ebony on the top of which perched an enormous black, short-haired cat, with yellow eyes, which, at first, indeed, until the animal made a slight movement, I took to be an objet d'art. Then Peter called, Lou Matagot, and with one magnificent bound, the creature landed on the silver table and arched his glossy back. Then he sharpened his claws and stretched his joints by the aid of the casket scratched with the cuneiform symbols.

Lou Matagot, Peter explained, signifies the Cat of Dreams, the Cat of the Sorcerers, in the Provençal dialect.

There were a few chairs, strangely modern, Ballet Russe chairs, upholstered in magenta and green and orange brocades in which were woven circles and crescents and stars of gold and silver, but Peter and I seated ourselves at one end of the room on a high purple couch, a sort of throne, piled with silver and black cushions, on which was worked in green threads an emblem, which Peter explained was the character of Mersilde, a fiend who has the power to transport you wherever you wish to go. Now, he pulled a silver rope which hung from the ceiling, the lights flashed off and on again, and I observed that we were no longer alone. A little black page boy in a rose doublet, with baggy silver trousers, and a turban of scarlet silk, surmounted by heron's plumes, sparkling with carbuncles, stood before us. He had apparently popped out of the floor like the harlequin in an English pantomime. At a sign from Peter, he pressed a button in the wall, a little cupboard opened, and he extracted a bottle of amber crystal, half-full of a clear green liquid, and two amber crystal glasses with iridescent flanges.

I am striving to discover the secrets, said Peter, as we sipped the liqueur, the taste of which was both pungent and bitter.

Not in this room! I gasped. Unless you mean the secrets of Paul Poiret and Léon Bakst.

No, he laughed, as the cat leaped to his shoulder and began to purr loudly, not in this room. This is my reception-room where I receive nobody. You are the first person, with the exception of Hadji, to enter this house since I have remodelled it but, he continued reflectively, I have a fancy that the bright fiends of hell, the beautiful yellow and blue devils, will like this room, when I call them forth to do my bidding.

Again he warned me, Not one word to Edith, do you understand? Not one word. I must be alone. I have told you and only you. I must work in peace and that I cannot do if I am interrupted. This room is my relief. It amuses me to sit here, but it is not my laboratory. Come, it is time to show you. Besides, I have my reasons. . .

We did not rise. The lights were again mysteriously extinguished and I felt that the couch on which we sat was moving. The sensation was pleasant, like taking a ride on a magic carpet or a taktrevan. In a few seconds, when light appeared again, instead of a wall behind us we sat with a wall before us. Facing about, I perceived that we were in another chamber, a chamber that would have pleased Doctor Faust, for it was obviously the laboratory of an alchemist. Nevertheless, I noted at once a certain theatrical air in the arrangement.

This, I said, seems more suitable for the performances of Herrmann the Great or Houdini than the experiments of Paracelsus.

Peter grinned. It was clear that he was taking a childish delight in the entertainment.

It *is* fun to do this with you. I've had no one but the black boy and the cat. There are moments when I think I would like to bring Edith here, but she would spoil it by getting tired of it, or else she would like it too much and want to come every day and bring others with her to see the show. Well, look around.

I followed his advice. It was the conventional alchemist's retreat. There were stuffed owls and mummies and astrolabes. Herbs and bones were suspended from the ceiling. Skulls grinned from the tops of cabinets. There were rows and rows of ancient books, many of them bound in sheepskin or vellum, in a case against one wall. A few larger volumes, with brass or iron clasps, reposed on a table. Lou Matagot, who had been carried into the room with us, presently stretched his great, black, glossy length over the top of one of these. There were cauldrons, retorts, crucibles, rows of bottles, a fire, with bellows, and a clepsydra, or water-clock, which seemed to be running. There was an Arcula Mystica, or demoniac telephone, resembling a liqueur-stand. Peter explained that possessors of this instrument might communicate with each other, over whatever distance. There were cabinets, on the shelves of which lay amulets and talismans and periapts, carved from obsidian or fashioned of blue or green faience, the surfaces of which were elaborately scratched with hermetic characters, and symplegmata with their curious confusion of the different parts of different beasts. There were aspergills, and ivory pyxes, stolen, perhaps, from some holy place, and now consecrated to evil uses. There were stuffed serpents and divining rods of hazel. There were scrolls of parchment, tied with vermilion cord. In fact, there was everything in this room, that David Belasco would provide for a similar scene on the stage.

Here, said Peter, I study the Book of the Dead, hierograms, rhabdomancy, oneiromancy, hippomancy, margaritomancy, parthenomancy, gyromancy, spodanomancy, ichthyomancy, kephalonomancy, lampodomancy, sycomancy, angelology, pneumatology, goety, eschatology, cartomancy, aleuromancy, alphitomancy, anthropomancy, axinomancy, which is performed by applying an agate to a red-hot ax, arithmomancy, or divination by numbers, alectoromantia, in which I lay out the letters of the alphabet and grains of wheat in spaces drawn in a circle and permit a cock to select grains corresponding to letters, belomancy, divination by arrows, ceroscopy, cleidomancy, astragalomancy, amniomancy, cleromancy, divination performed by throwing dice and observing the marks which turn up, cledonism, coscinomancy, capnomancy, divination by smoke, captoptromancy, chiromancy, dactyliomancy, performed with a ring, extispicium, or divination by entrails, gastromancy, geomancy, divination by earth, hydromancy, divination by water, and pyromancy and æromancy, divination by fire and air, onomancy, divination by the letters of a name, onychomancy, which is concerned with fingernails, ornithomancy, which deals with birds, and chilomancy, which deals with keys, lithomancy, eychnomancy, ooscopy, keraunoscopia, bibliomancy, myomancy, pan-psychism, metempsychosis, the Martinists, the Kabbalists, the Diabolists, the Palladists, the Rosicrucians, the Luciferians, the Umbilicamini, all the nocuous, demonological, and pneumatic learning, including transcendental sensualism. At present, I am experimenting with white mice. I dip their feet in red ink and permit them to make scrawls on a certain curious chart.

I have dabbled in drugs, for you know that the old Greek priests, the modern seers, and the mediæval pythonesses, all have resorted to drugs to assist them to see visions. The narcotic or anæsthetic fumes, rising from the tripods, lulled the old Greek hierophants and soothsayers into a sympathetic frame of mind. First, I experimented with Napellus, for I had read that Napellus caused one's mental processes to be transferred from the brain to the pit of the stomach. There exists an exact description of the effects of this drug on an adept, one Baptista Van Helmont, which I will read you.

Peter, here, went to the shelves, and after a little hesitation, pulled out an old brown volume. He turned over the pages for a few seconds and then began to read: Once, when I had prepared the root (of Napellus) in a rough manner, I tasted it with the tongue: although I had swallowed nothing, and had spit out a good deal of the juice, yet I felt as if my skull was being compressed by a string. Several household matters suggested themselves and I went about the house and attended to them. At last, I experienced what I had never felt before. It seemed to me that I neither thought nor understood, and as if I had none of the usual ideas in my head; but I felt, with astonishment, clearly and distinctly, that all these functions were taking place at the pit of the stomach: I felt this clearly and perfectly, and observed with the greatest attention that, although I felt movement and sensation spreading themselves over the whole body, yet that the whole power of thought was really and unmistakably situated in the pit of the stomach, always excepting a sensation that the soul was in the brain as a governing force. The sensation was beyond the power of words to describe. I perceived that I thought with greater clearness: there was a pleasure in such an intellectual distinctness. It was not a fugitive sensation; it did not take place while I slept, dreamed, or was ill, but during perfect consciousness. I perceived clearly that the head was perfectly dormant as regarded fancy: and I felt not a little astonished at the change of position.

Well, continued Peter, closing the book and regarding me with great intensity, you will admit that would be a sensation worth experiencing. So I tried it. . . with horrible results. Will you believe it when I tell you that I became wretchedly ill in that very centre which Van Helmont locates as the seat of thought? I suffered from the most excruciating pains, which were not entirely relieved by an emetic. Indeed, I passed a week or so in bed.

My next experiment, he went on, was made with hashish, Cannabis Indica, which I prepared and took according to the directions of another adept, who had found that the drug produced a kind of demoniac and incessant laughter, hearty, Gargantuan laughter, and the foreshortening of time and space. He could span the distance between London and Paris in a few seconds. Furniture and statues assumed a comic attitude; they seemed to move about and become familiar with him. He was literally aware of what the Rosny have called the "semi-humanité des choses." I took the drug, as I have said, exactly as he directed, but the effect on me was entirely dissimilar. Immediately, I was plunged into immoderate melancholy. The sight of any object immeasurably depressed me. I also noted that my legs and arms had apparently stretched to an abnormal length. I sobbed with despair when I discovered that I could scarcely see to the other end of my laboratory, it seemed so far away. Mounting the stairs to my bed-chamber was equivalent in my mind to climbing the Himalayas. Although Hadji afterward assured me that I had been under the influence of the drug for only fourteen hours, it was more like fourteen years to me, which I had passed without sleep. At the end of the experiment, my nerves revolted under the strain and again I was forced to take to my bed, this time for four days.

My third experiment was made with Peyote beans, whose properties are extolled by the American Indians. After eating these beans, the red men, who use them in the mysteries of their worship, suffer, I have been informed, from an excruciating nausea, the duration of which is prolonged. After the nausea has passed its course, a series of visions is vouchsafed the experimenter, these visions extending in a series, on various planes, to the mystic number of seven. Under the spell of these visions, the adepts vaticinate future events. I have wondered sometimes if it were not possible that the ancient Egyptians were familiar with the properties of these beans, that William Blake was under their influence when he drew his mystic plates.

Be that as it may, I swallowed one bean, which I had been informed would be sufficient to give me the desired effect, and without interval, I was carried at once on to the plane of the visions, which concentrated themselves into one gigantic phantasm. Have you ever seen Jacques Callot's copperplate engraving of The Temptation of Saint Anthony? The hideous collection of teratological monsters, half-insect, half-microbe, of gigantic size, exposed in that picture, swarmed about me, menacing me with their horrid beaks, their talons and claws, their evil antennæ. Further cohorts of malignant monstrosities without bones lounged about the room and sprawled against my body, rubbing their flabby, slimy, oozing folds against my legs. After a few more stercoraceous manœuvres, some of which I should hesitate to describe, even to you, the monsters began to breathe forth liquid fire, and the pain resulting from the touch of these tongues of flame finally awoke me. I was violently ill, and my illness developed in the seven stages traditionally allotted to the visions. First, extreme nausea, which lasted for two days, second, a raging fever, third, a procession of green eruptions on my legs, fourth, terrific pains in the region of my abdomen, fifth, dizziness, sixth, inability to command any of my muscles, and seventh, a prolonged period of sleep, which lasted for forty-eight hours. Nevertheless, I came nearer to success in this experiment than in any other.

My fourth experiment was made with cocaine, which I procured from a little Italian boy, about eleven years old, who was acting in a Bowery barroom as agent for his father. Laying the white crystals on the blade of an ivory paper-cutter, I sniffed as I had observed the snow-birds themselves sniff. Immediately, my mind became clear to an extent that it had never been clear before. My intellect became as sharp as a knife, as keen as the slash of a whip, as vibrant as an E string. I seemed to have a power of understanding which I had never before approached, not only of understanding but also of *hearing*, for I caught the conversation of men talking in an ordinary tone of voice out in the Square. Also, I became abnormally active, nervous, and intense. I rushed from the room, without reason or purpose, with a kind of energy which seemed deathless, so strong was its power. When, however, I endeavoured to make notes, for my mind seethed with ideas, I was unable to do so. I scratched some characters on paper, to be sure, but I found them wholly undecipherable the next day. They were not in English or in any language known to me. Finally, I ran out of the house and, encountering, on Second Avenue, a fancy woman of the Jewish persuasion, I accompanied her to her cubicle, and permitted her to be the subsidiary hierophant in the mystic rites I then performed.

That, concluded Peter, with a somewhat sorry smile, was the last of my experiments with drugs.

This story and, indeed, this whole phase, amused me enormously. An ambition which had persuaded its possessor that in order to become the American Arthur Machen, he must first become an adept in demonology seemed to me to be the culmination of Peter's fantastic life, which, indeed, it was. But I said little. As usual, I let him talk and I listened. There seemed, however, to be a period here and I took occasion to look over the books, asking him first if he had any objection to my copying off some of the titles, as I felt that it might be possible that some day I should want to make some research in this esoteric realm. He bade me do what I liked and, advancing towards the book-shelves with the small note-book which I carried with me at that period in order to set down fleeting thoughts as they came, I transferred some of the titles therein.

I stopped at last, not from lack of patience on my part, but from observing the impatience of Peter, who obviously had a good deal more to say. On my turning, indeed, he began at once.

I have made, he said, some tentative minor experiments but my final experiments are yet to be attempted. Nevertheless, I have found a springboard from which to leap into my romance. Let me read you a few pages of Arthur Waite's somewhat ironic summary of Dr. Bataille's Le Diable au XIX Siècle. Naturally I shall treat the subject more seriously, but what atmosphere, what a gorgeous milieu in which to plunge the reader when he shall open my book!

Peter now took from the shelves a small black volume, lettered in red, and turned over the leaves. First, he said, I shall read you some of the Doctor's experiences in Pondicherry, and he began:

Through the greenery of a garden, the gloom of a well, and the entanglement of certain stairways, they entered a great dismantled temple, devoted to the service of Brahma, under the unimpressive diminutive of Lucif. The infernal sanctuary had a statue of Baphomet, identical with that in Ceylon, and the ill-ventilated place reeked with a horrible putrescence. Its noisome condition was mainly owing to the presence of various fakirs, who, though still alive, were in advanced stages of putrefaction. Most people are supposed to go easily and pleasantly to the devil, but these elected to do so by way of a charnel-house asceticism, and an elaborate system of self-torture. Some were suspended from the ceiling by a rope tied to their arms, some embedded in plaster, some stiffened in a circle, some permanently distorted into the shape of the letter S; some were head downwards, some in a cruciform position. A native Grand Master explained that they had postured for years in this manner, and one of them for a quarter of a century.

Fr∴ John Campbell proceeded to harangue the assembly in Ourdou-zaban, but the doctor comprehended completely, and reports the substance of his speech, which was violently anti-Catholic in its nature, and especially directed against missionaries. This finished, they proceeded to the evocation of Baal-Zeboub, at first by the Conjuration of the Four, but no fiend appeared. The operation was repeated ineffectually a second time, and John Campbell determined upon the Grand Rite, which began by each person spinning on his own axis, and in this manner circumambulating the temple, in procession. Whenever they passed an embedded fakir, they obtained an incantation from his lips, but still Baal-Zeboub failed. Thereupon, the native Grand Master suggested that the evocation should be performed by the holiest of all fakirs, who was produced from a cupboard more fetid than the temple itself, and proved to be in the following condition:—(a) face eaten by rats; (b) one bleeding eye hanging down by his mouth; (c) legs covered with gangrene, ulcers, and rottenness; (d) expression peaceful and happy.

Entreated to call on Baal-Zeboub, each time he opened his mouth his eye fell into it; however, he continued the invocation, but no Baal-Zeboub manifested. A tripod of burning coals was next obtained, and a woman, summoned for this purpose, plunged her arm into the flames, inhaling with great delight the odour of her roasting flesh. Result, *nil*. Then a white goat was produced, placed upon the altar of Baphomet, set alight, hideously tortured, cut open, and its entrails torn out by the native Grand Master, who spread them on the steps, uttering abominable blasphemies against Adonaï. This having also failed, great stones were raised from the floor, a nameless stench ascended, and a large consignment of living fakirs, eaten to the bone by worms and falling to pieces in every direction, were dragged out from among a number of skeletons, while serpents, giant spiders, and toads swarmed from all parts. The Grand Master seized one of the fakirs and cut his throat upon the altar, chanting the satanic liturgy amidst imprecations, curses, a chaos of voices, and the last agonies of the goat. The blood spirted forth upon the assistants, and the Grand Master sprinkled the Baphomet. A final howl of invocation resulted in complete failure, whereupon it was decided that Baal-Zeboub had business elsewhere.

The doctor departed from the ceremony and kept his bed for eight-and-forty hours.

Peter looked up from the book in his hand with an expression of ironic exultation which was very quaint.

What do you think of that? he asked.

Very pretty, I ventured.

Very strong for the beginning of my romance! he cried. You see, I shall commence with this failure and work up gradually to the final brilliant success. Let me introduce you to another passage from Waite's summary of Dr. Bataille's masterpiece: He turned a few more leaves and presently was reading again:

A select company of initiates proceeded in hired carriages through the desolation of Dappah, under the convoy of the initiated coachmen, for the operation of a great satanic solemnity. At an easy distance from the city is the Sheol of the native Indians, and hard by the latter place there is a mountain 500 feet high and 2000 long on the summit of which seven temples are erected, communicating one with another by subterranean passages in the rock. The total absence of pagodas makes it evident that these temples are devoted to the worship of Satan; they form a gigantic triangle superposed on the vast plateau, at the base of which the party descended from their conveyances, and were met by a native with an accommodating knowledge of French. Upon exchanging the Sign of Lucifer, he conducted them to a hole in the rock, which gave upon a narrow passage guarded by a line of Sikhs with drawn swords, prepared to massacre anybody, and leading to the vestibule of the first temple, which was filled with a miscellaneous concourse of Adepts. In the first temple, which was provided with the inevitable statue of Baphomet, but was withal bare and meagrely illuminated, the doctor was destined to pass through his promised ordeal for which he was stripped to the skin, and placed in the centre of the assembly, and at a given signal one thousand odd venomous cobra de capellos were produced from holes in the wall and encouraged to fold him in their embraces, while the music of flute-playing fakirs alone intervened to prevent his instant death. He passed through this trying encounter with a valour which amazed himself, persisted in prolonging the ceremony, and otherwise proved himself a man of such extraordinary metal that he earned universal respect. From the Sanctuary of the Serpents, the company then proceeded into the second temple or the Sanctuary of the Phœnix.

The second temple was brilliantly illuminated and ablaze with millions of precious stones wrested by the wicked English from innumerable conquered Rajahs; it had garlands of diamonds, festoons of rubies, vast images of solid silver, and a gigantic Phœnix in red gold more solid than the silver. There was an altar beneath the Phœnix, and a male and female ape were composed on the altar steps, while the Grand Master proceeded to the celebration of a black mass, which was followed by an amazing marriage of the two engaging animals, and the sacrifice of a lamb brought alive into the temple, bleating piteously, with nails driven through its feet.

The third temple was consecrated to the Mother of fallen women, who, in memory of the adventure of the apple, has a place in the calendar of Lucifer; the proceedings consisted of a dialogue between the Grand Master and the Vestal.

The fourth temple was a Rosicrucian Sanctuary, having an open sepulchre, from which blue flames continually emanated; there was a platform in the midst of the temple designed for the accommodation of more Indian Vestals, one of whom it was proposed should evaporate into thin air, after which a fakir would be transformed before the company into a living mummy and be interred for a space of three years. The fakir introduced his performance by suspension in mid-air.

The fifth temple was consecrated to the Pelican.

The sixth temple was that of the Future and was devoted to divinations, the oracles being given by a Vestal in a hypnotic condition, seated over a burning brazier.

The assembly now thoughtfully repaired to the seventh temple, which, being sacred to Fire, was equipped with a vast central furnace surmounted by a chimney and containing a gigantic statue of Baphomet; in spite of the intolerable heat pervading the entire chamber, this idol contrived to preserve its outlines and to glow without pulverizing. A ceremony of an impressive nature occurred in this apartment; a wild cat, which strayed in through the open window, was regarded as the appearance of a soul in transmigration, and in spite of its piteous protests, was passed through the fire to Baal.

And now the crowning function, the Magnum Opus of the mystery, must take place in the Sheol of Dappah; a long procession filed from the mountain temples to the charnel-house of the open plain; the night was dark, the moon had vanished in dismay, black clouds scudded across the heavens, a feverish rain fell slowly at intervals, and the ground was dimly lighted by the phosphorescence of the general putrefaction. The Adepts stumbled over dead bodies, disturbing rats and vultures, and proceeded to the formation of the magic chain, sitting in a vast circle, every Adept embracing his particular corpse.

Well? asked Peter, closing the book. Well?

Kolossal! I shouted, in German.

Isn't it, and there's ever so much more, wonderful stories, incantations and evocations in the works of Arthur Waite, Moncure Daniel Conway, Alfred Maury, J. Collin de Plancy, François Lenormant, Alphonse Gallais, the Abbé de Montfaucon de Villars, J. G. Bourgeat, and William Godwin. Have you ever heard of The Black Pullet or The Queen of The Hairy Flies?

This time, Carl; he spoke with great intensity and earnestness, I am on the right track. I am convinced that to give a work of this character a proper background one must know a great deal more than one tells. That, in fact, is the secret of all fine literature, the secret of all great art, that it conceals and suggests. The edges, of course, are rounded: it is not a rough and obvious concealment. You cannot begin not to tell until you know more than you are willing to impart. These books have given me a good deal, but I must go farther—as I am convinced that Machen has gone farther. I am going through with it. . . all through with it, searching out the secrets of life and death, a few of which I have discovered already, but I have yet to make the great test. And when I know what I shall find out, I shall begin to write. . . but I shall tell nothing.

Peter was flaming with enthusiasm again. It wasn't necessary for me to speak. He required an audience, not an interlocutor.

Why not now? he demanded suddenly. Why not now and here, with you?

What do you mean? I queried.

Why not make the great experiment now? I am prepared and the moon and the planets are favourable. Are *you* willing to go through with it? I must warn you that you will never be the same again. You may even lose your life.

What will happen? I asked.

The earth will rock. A storm will probably follow, thunder and lightning, balls of fire, thunder-bolts, showers of feathers, and then we shall dissolve into. . . into a putrid mass, the agamous mass from which we originated, neither male nor female, with only a glowing eye, a great eye, radiating intelligence out of its midst. Then Astaroth himself (I shall call Astaroth, because his inferiors in the descending hierarchy, Sargatanas and Nebiros, dwell in America) will appear, in one of his forms, perhaps refulgent and beautiful, perhaps ugly and tortured and hideously deformed, perhaps black or yellow or blue, but assuredly not white or green. He may be entirely covered with hair or entirely covered with eyes, or he may be eyeless. Mayhap, he will be lean and proud and sad, and he will probably limp, for you know he is lame. His feet will be cloven, he will wear a goat's beard, and you may distinguish him further by the cock's feather and the ox's tail. Or, perhaps, he may arrive in the shape of some monster: the fierce flying hydra called the Ouranabad, the Rakshe who eats dragons and snakes, the Soham, with the body of a scarlet griffin and the head of a four-eyed horse, the Syl, a basilisk with a human face. . . But, however he may appear, in his presence you shall learn the last secrets of all the worlds.

And then what will happen?

Then I shall speak the magic formula and we will resume our proper shapes but from that moment on we shall hover—literally, not pathologically—between life and death. We shall know everything. . . and eventually we shall pay the price. . .

Like Faust?

Like Faust. . . that is, if we are not clever enough to outwit the demon. Those who practise devilments usually find some means to circumvent the devil.

I appeared to ponder.

I am willing to go through with it, I said at last.

Good! I knew you would be. Let's get to work at once!

He lifted the most ponderous volume in the laboratory from the floor to the top of an old walnut refectory table. The book was bound in musty yellow vellum, clasped with iron, and the foxed leaves were fashioned from parchment made from the skin of virgin camels. As he opened it, I saw that the pages were inscribed with cabalistic characters and symbols, illuminated in colours, none of which I could decipher. Lou Matagot jumped on to the table and sat on the leaves at the top of the book, forming a paper weight. He sat with his back to Peter and his long, black tail played nervously up and down the centre of the volume.

Peter now drew a circle with a radius of twelve or thirteen feet around us, inscribing within its circumference certain characters and pentacles. Then he plunged a dagger through what I recognized to be a sacred wafer, which he told me had been stolen from a church at midnight, at the same time, muttering what, from the tone of his voice, I took to be blasphemous imprecations, although the language he used was unfamiliar to me. Next he arranged a copper chafing-dish over a blue flame and began to stir the ingredients, esoteric powders and crystals of bright colours. Now he lovingly lifted a crystal viol, filled with a purple liquid, and poured the contents into a porcelain bowl. Instantly, there was a faint detonation and a thick cloud of violet vapour mounted spirally to the ceiling. All the time, occasionally referring to the grimoire on the table, and employing certain unmentionable symbolic objects in the manner prescribed, he muttered incantations in the unknown tongue. The room swam with odours and mists, violet clouds and opopanax fogs. So far, the invocation was pretty and amusing but it resembled the arcane rites of Paul Iribe more than those of Hermes Trismegistus.

Now Peter pulled three black hairs from the cat's tail, which Lou Matagot delivered with a yowl of rage, springing at the same time from the table to the top of the cabinet, whence he regarded us through the mists and vapours, with his evil yellow eyes. The hairs went into the chafing-dish and a new aroma filled the room. The claws of an owl, the flower of the moly, and the powder of vipers followed and then Peter opened a long flat box which nearly covered one end of the huge table, and a nest of serpents, with bellies of rich turquoise blue and backs of tawny yellow, marked with black zigzags, reared their wicked heads. He called them by name and they responded by waving their heads rhythmically. I began to grow alarmed and dizzy. Vade retro, Satanas! was on tip of my tongue. For a few seconds, I think, I must have fainted. When I revived, I still heard the chanting of the incantation and the sound of tinkling bells. The serpents' heads still waved in rhythm and their bodies, yellow and turquoise blue, were elongated in the air until they appeared to be balancing on the tips of their tails. The eyes of Lou Matagot glared maliciously through the thick vapours and the cat howled with rage or terror.

Now! cried Peter, for the first time in English. Now!

My nails dug holes in the palms of my perspiring hands. Peter renewed his nocuous muttering and casting the wafer, transfixed by the dagger, into the porcelain bowl containing the violet fluid, he poured the whole mixture into the copper chafing-dish.

There was a terrific explosion.

CARL VAN VECHTEN

XI

I left the hospital before Peter. My injuries, indeed, were of so slight a nature that I was confined only a few days, while his were so serious that the physicians despaired of his life, and he was forced to keep to his bed for several months. Following my early discharge, I made daily visits of inquiry to the hospital but it was not until June, 1914, that I was assured that he would recover. With this good news, came a certain sense of relief, and I made plans for another voyage to Europe. The incidents of that voyage—I was in Paris at the beginning of the war—are of sufficient interest so that I may recount them in another place, but they bear no relationship to the present narrative.

Subsequent to his recovery, I have learned since from the physician who attended him during his protracted illness, Peter returned to Toledo with his mother. It is probable that he made further literary experiments. It has even occurred to me that the pivot of his being, the explanation for his whole course of action may have escaped me. Although, from the hour of our first meeting, my interest in and my affection for Peter were deep, assuredly I never imagined that I should be writing down the history of his life. For the greater part of the term of our friendship, indeed, I was a writer only in a very modest sense. I was not on the lookout for the kind of "copy" his affairs and ideas offered, for at this period I was a reporter of music and the drama. Even later, when I began to set down my thoughts in what is euphemistically called a more permanent form, the notion of using Peter as a subject never presented itself to me, and if he had asked me to do so during his lifetime, urging me to put aside a pile of unfinished work in his behalf, the request would have astounded me. I made, therefore, no special effort to ferret out his secrets. When it was convenient for both of us we met and, largely by accident, I was a silent witness of three of his literary experiments. How many others he may have made, I do not know. It is possible that at some time or other he may have been inspired by the religious school, the Tolstoy theory of art, or he may have followed the sensuous lead of Gozzoli and Debussy, artists whose work intrigued him enormously, or in another æsthetic avatar, he may have believed that true art is degrading or coldly classic. There is even the possibility, by no means remote, that he may have fallen under the influence of the small-town and psychoanalytic schools. Except in a general way, however, in a conversation which I shall record at the end of this chapter, he never mentioned further experiments. It is possible that others may have evidence bearing on this point. Martha Baker might make a good witness, but she died in 1911. Mrs. Whiffle knew nothing of any importance whatever about her son. Since his death I have interrogated her in vain. She was, indeed, very much astonished at the little I told her and she will read this book, I think, with real amazement. The report of Clara Barnes, too, was negligible. Edith Dale has supplied me with a few facts which I have inserted where they chronologically belong. Most of my other friends, Phillip Moeller, Alfred Knopf, Edna Kenton, Pitts Sanborn, Avery Hopwood, Freddo Sides, Joseph Hergesheimer, even my wife, Fania Marinoff, never met Peter. Louis Sherwin walked up Fifth Avenue with us one day, but Peter was unusually silent and after he had left us at the corner of Fifty-seventh Street, Louis was not sufficiently curious to ask any questions concerning him. I doubt if Louis could even recall the incident today. I have inserted advertisements in the Paris, New York, and Toledo newspapers, begging any one with pertinent facts or letters in his possession to communicate with me, but as yet I have received no replies. I have never seen a photograph of my friend and his mother informs me that she doubts if he ever sat for one.

The record, therefore, of Peter's literary life, at the conclusion of this chapter, will be as complete as I can make it. I have tried to set down the truth as I saw it, leaving out nothing that I remember, even at the danger of becoming unnecessarily garrulous and rambling. I have written down all I know because, after all, I may have misunderstood or misinterpreted, and some one else, with the facts before him, may be better able to reconstruct the picture of this strange life.

Our next meeting occurred in January, 1919, and his first remark was, Thank God, you're not shot up! From that time, until the day of his death, nearly a year later, Peter never mentioned the war to me again, although I saw him frequently enough, nor did he speak of his writing, save once, on an occasion which shall be reported in its proper place.

When we came together for the first time, after the long interval— he had just returned to New York from Florida—I was surprised at and even shocked by the purely physical change, which, to be sure, had a psychical significance, for his face had grown more spiritual. He had always been slender, but now he was thin, almost emaciated. To describe his appearance a little later, I might use the word haggard. His coat, which once fitted his figure snugly, rather hung from his shoulders. There were white patches in the blue-black of his hair, deep circles under his eyes, and hollows in his cheeks. But his eyes, themselves, seemed to shine with a new light, seemed to see something which I could not even imagine. He had rid himself of many excrescences and externalities, the purely adscititious qualities, charming though they might be, which masked his personality. He had, indeed, discovered himself, although I never knew how clearly until our last conversation. Peter, without appearing to be particularly aware of it, had become a mystic. His emancipation had come through suffering. He was quieter, less restless, less excitable, still enthusiastic, but with more balance, more—I do not wish to be misunderstood—irony. He had found life very satisfying and very hard, very sweet, with something of a bitter after-taste. He seemed almost holy to me, reminding me at times of those ascetic monks who crawl two thousand miles on their bellies to worship at some shrine, or of those Hindu fakirs who lie in one tortured position for years, their bodies slowly consuming, while their souls gain fire. That he was ill, very ill, I surmised at once, although, like everything else I have noted here, this was an impression. He made no admissions, never spoke of his malady; indeed, for Peter, he talked astonishingly little about himself. He was pathetic and at the same time an object for admiration.

Afterwards, I learned from his mother that he suffered from an incurable disease, the disease that killed him late in 1919. But he never spoke of this to me and he never complained, unless his occasional confession that he was tired might be construed as a complaint.

We had fine times together, of a new kind. The tables, in a sense, were turned. I had become the writer, however humble, and his ambition had not been realized. His sympathy with my work, with what I was trying to do, which he saw almost immediately, saw, indeed, in the beginning, more clearly than I saw it myself, was complete. He was never weary of talking about it, at any rate he never showed me that he was weary, and naturally this drew us very closely together, for an author is fondest of those men who talk the most about his work. But this is not the place to publish his opinions of me, although some of them were so curious and farseeing—they were not all flattering by any means—that I shall undoubtedly recur to them in my autobiography. Fortunately for me, his sympathy grew as my work progressed, and it seemed amazing to me later, looking over the book after a period of years, that he had found anything pleasant to report of Music After the Great War. He had, indeed, seen something in it, and when I recalled what he had said it was impossible to feel that he had overstated the case in the interests of friendship. He had seen the germ, the root of what was to come; he had seen a suggestion of a style, undeveloped ideas, which he felt would later be developed, as indeed, to a limited extent, they were. His plea, to put it concisely, had been for a more personal expression. He was always asking me, after this or that remark or anecdote in conversation, why I did not write it, just as I had said it or told it, and it was a great pleasure for him to perceive in The Merry-Go-Round and In the Garret (of which he read the proofs just before his death) some signs of growth in this direction.

You are becoming freer, he would say. You are loosening your tongue; your heart is beating faster. In time you may liberate those subconscious ideas which are entangled in your very being. It is only your conscious self that prevents you from becoming a really interesting writer. Let that once be as free as the air and the *other* will be free too. You must walk boldly and proudly and without fear. You must search the heart; the mind is negligible in literature as in all other forms of art. Try to write just as you feel and you will discover that your feeling is greater than your knowledge of it. The words that appear on the paper will at first seem strange to you, almost like hermetic symbols, and it is possible that in the course of time you will be able to say so much that you yourself will not understand what you are writing. Do not be afraid of that. Let the current flow freely when you feel that it is the true current that is flowing.

That is the lesson, he continued, that the creative or critical artist can learn from the interpreter, the lesson of the uses of personality. The great interpreters, Rachel, Ristori, Mrs. Siddons, Duse, Bernhardt, Réjane, Ysaye, Paderewski, and Mary Garden are all big, vibrant personalities, that the deeper thing, call it God, call it IT, flows through and permeates. You may not believe this now, but I *know* it is true, and you will know it yourself some day. And if you cannot release your personality, what you write, though it be engraved in letters an inch deep on stones weighing many tons, will lie like snow in the street to be melted away by the first rain.

We talked of other writers. Peter drew my attention, for instance, to the work of Cunninghame Graham, that strange Scotch mystic who turned his back on civilization to write of the pampas, the arid plains of Africa, India, and Spain, only to find irony everywhere in every work of man. But, observed Peter, he could not hate civilization so intensely had he not lived in it. It is all very well to kick over the ladder after you have climbed it and set foot on the balcony. Like all lovers of the simple life, he is very complex. And we discussed James Branch Cabell, who, Peter told me, was originally a "romantic." He wrote of knights and ladyes and palfreys with sympathetic picturesqueness. Of late, however, continued Peter, he, too, seems to have turned over in bed. Romanticism still appears in his work but it is undermined by a biting and disturbing irony. He asks: Are any of the manifestations of modern civilization worthy of admiration? and like Graham, he seems to answer, No. It is possible that the public disregard for his earlier and simpler manner may have produced this metamorphosis. Many a man has become bitter with less reason. Then he spoke of the attributed influence of Maurice Hewlett and Anatole France on the work of Cabell. Bernard Shaw, said Peter, once lost all patience with those critics who insisted that he was a son of Ibsen and Nietzsche and asserted that it was their ignorance that prevented them from realizing the debt he owed to Samuel Butler. Cabell might, with justice, voice a similar complaint, for if he ever had a literary father it was Arthur Machen. In that author's The Chronicle of Clemendy, issued in 1888, may be discovered the same confusion of irony and romance that is to be traced in the work of Cabell. Moreover, like The Soul of Melicent, the book purports to be a translation from an old chronicle. I might further speak of the relationship between Hieroglyphics and Beyond Life, The Hill of Dreams and The Cream of the Jest, although in each case the treatment and the style are entirely dissimilar. Machen even preceded Cabell in his use of unfavourable reviews (Vide the advertising pages of Beyond Life) in his preface to the 1916 edition of The Great God Pan. Perhaps, added Peter, Cabell has also read Herman Melville's Mardi to some advantage. But he is no plagiarist; I am speaking from the point of view of literary genealogy. Peter, at my instigation, read a novel or two of Joseph Hergesheimer's. Linda Condon, he reported, is as evanescent as the spirit of God. Only those who have encountered Lady Beauty among the juniper trees in the early dawn will *feel* this book, and only those who feel will understand. For Hergesheimer has worked a miracle; he has brought marble to life, created a vibrant chastity: He has described ice in words of flame!

One night, quite accidentally, we saw the name of Clara Barnes on a poster in front of the Metropolitan Opera House. She was singing the rôle of the Priestess in Aida. We purchased two general admission tickets and slipped in to hear her. The Priestess, those who have heard Aida will remember, officiates in the temple scene of the first act but, like the impersonator of the Bird in Siegfried, she is invisible. Clara's voice sounded tired and worn, as indeed, it should sound after those long years of study.

We must go back to see her, Peter urged.

We found a changed and broken Clara. She was dressing alone, but on the third floor, and the odour of Cœur de Jeannette persisted. She burst into tears when she saw us.

I can't do it, she moaned. Why did you ever come? I can't do it. I can only sing with my music in front of me. I shall never be able to sing a part which *appears* and there are so few rôles in opera, which permit you to sing back of the scenery! I can't remember. Now she was wailing. As fast as I learn one part I forget another.

As we walked away on Fortieth Street, Peter began to relate an incident he had once read in Plutarch: There was a certain magpie, belonging to a barber at Rome, which could imitate any word he heard. One day, a company of passing soldiers blew their trumpets before the shop and for the next forty-eight hours the magpie was not only mute but also pensive and melancholy. It was generally believed that the sound of the trumpets had stunned the bird and deprived it of both voice and hearing. It appeared, however, that this was not the case for, says Plutarch, the bird had all the time been occupied in profound meditation, studying how to imitate the sound of the trumpets, and when at last master of the trick, he astonished his friends by a perfect imitation of the flourish on those instruments it had heard, observing with the greatest exactness all the repetitions, stops, and changes. This lesson, however, had apparently been learned at the cost of the whole of its intelligence, for it made it forget everything it had learned before.

We visited many out-of-the-way places together, Peter and I, the Negro dance-halls near 135th Street, and the Italian and the Yiddish Theatres. Peter once remarked that he enjoyed plays more in a foreign language with which he was unfamiliar. What he could imagine of plot and dialogue far transcended the actuality. We often dined at a comfortable Italian restaurant on Spring Street, on the walls of which birds fluttered through frescoed arbours, trailing with fruits and flowers, and where the spaghetti was too good to be eaten without prayer. In an uptown café, we had a strange adventure with a Frenchwoman, La

Tigresse, which I have related elsewhere.[1] Peter refused, in these last months, to go to concerts, especially in Carnegie Hall, the atmosphere of which, he said, made it impossible to listen to music. The bare walls, the bright lights, the sweating conductors, and the silly, gaping crowd oppressed his spirit. He envied Ludwig of Bavaria who could listen to music in a darkened hall in which he was the only auditor. Conditions were more favourable in the moving picture theatres. The bands, perhaps, did not play so well but the auditoriums were more subtly lighted, so that the figures of the audience did not intrude.

Peter was more of a recluse than ever. It had been impossible to persuade him to meet anybody since the Edith Dale days (Edith herself was now living in New Mexico and, owing to a slight misunderstanding, I had not seen or heard from her in five years). He was even sensitive and morbid on the subject. He made me promise, as a matter of fact, after the Louis Sherwin episode, that in case we encountered any of my friends in a restaurant or at a theatre, I would not introduce him. There was, I assured myself, a good reason for this. In these last days, Peter faded out in a crowd. He lost a good deal of his personality even in the presence of a third person. I begged him to go with me to Florine Stettheimer's studio to see her pictures, which I was sure would please him, but he refused. He liked to stroll around with me in odd places and he read and played the piano a good deal, but he seemed to have few other interests. He was absolutely ignorant of such matters as politics and government. He never voted and I have heard him refer to the president, and not in jest, as Abraham Wilson. Sports did not amuse him either, but occasionally we went together to see the wrestlers at Madison Square Garden, especially when Stanislaus Zbyszko was announced to appear.

He never went to Europe again although, shortly before he died, he talked of a voyage to Spain. He visited his mother at Toledo several times and he had planned a trip to Florida, the climate of which he found particularly soothing to his malady, in January, 1920. Occasionally he just disappeared, returning again, somewhat mysteriously, without any explanation, without, indeed, any admission that he had been away. I knew him too well to ask questions and, to say truth, there was something very sweet about these little mystifications. Privacy was so dear a privilege to him that even with his nearest friends, of which,

---

1. In the Garret.

assuredly, I was one, perhaps the nearest in this last year, it was essential to his happiness that he should maintain a certain restraint, a certain reserve, I had almost said, a certain mystery, but, curiously, there was nothing theatrical about Peter, even in his most theatrical performances. Just as by the fineness of his taste, Rembrandt softened the hideousness of a lurid subject in his Anatomy Lesson, so the exquisite charm of Peter's personality overcame any possible repugnance to anything he might choose to do.

During this last year in New York, he lived in an old house on Beekman Place, that splendid row, just two blocks long, of mellow brown-stone dwellings, with flights of steps, which back upon the East River at Fiftieth Street. We often sat on the balcony, looking over towards the span of the Queensboro Bridge, Blackwell's Island, with its turreted and battlemented castles so like the Mysteries of Udolpho, watching the gulls sweep over the surface of the water, the smoke wreathe from the factory chimneys, and the craft on the river, with cargoes "of Tyne coal, road-rails, pig-lead, fire-wood, iron-ware, and cheap tin trays," of the city, but seemingly away from it, with our backs to it, literally, indeed, while life ebbed by. And, at my side, too, I saw it slowly ebbing.

The interior, one of those fine old New York interiors, with high ceilings, bordered with plaster guilloches, white carved marble fire-places, sliding doors, and huge crystal chandeliers, whose pendants jingled when some one walked on the floor above, it had been his happy fancy to decorate in the early Victorian manner. The furniture, to be sure, was mostly Chippendale, Sheraton, and Heppelwhite, but there were also heavy carved walnut chairs, upholstered in lovely figured glazed chintzes. The mirrors were framed in four inches of purple and red engraved glass. The highboys were littered with ornaments, Staffordshire china dogs and shepherdesses, splendid feather and shell flowers, and ormolu clocks stood under glass bells on the mantelshelves. He had found a couple of rather worn, but still handsome, Aubusson carpets, with garlands of huge roses of a pale blush colour. One of these was in the drawing-room, the other in the library. An old sampler screen framed the fire-place in the latter room. The books were curious. Peter was now interested in byways of literature. I remember such volumes as Thomas Mann's Der Tod in Venedig, Paterne Berrichon's Life of Arthur Rimbaud, Alfred Jarry's Ubu Roi, with music by Claude Terrasse, Jean Lorrain's La Maison Philibert, Richard Garnett's The Twilight of the

Gods, the Comte de Lautréamont's Les Chants de Maldoror, Leolinus Siluriensis's The Anatomy of Tobacco, Binet-Valmer's Lucien, Haldane MacFall's The Wooings of Jezebel Pettyfer, James Morier's Hajji Baba of Ispahan, Robert Hugh Benson's The Necromancers, André Gide's L'Immoraliste, and various volumes by Guillaume Apollinaire. The walls of the drawing-room were hung with a French eighteenth century, rose cotton print, the design of which showed, on one side, Cupid rowing lustily, while listless old Time sat in the bow of the boat, with the motto: l'Amour fait passer le Temps; and, on the other side, Time propelling the boat, while a saddened Cupid, his face buried in his hands, was the downcast passenger, with the motto: Le Temps fait passer l'Amour. In the centre, beside a charming Greek temple, a nymph toyed with a spaniel, and the motto read: l'Amitié ne craint pas le Temps! There were, therefore, no pictures on these walls, but, elsewhere, where the walls were white, or where they were hung with rich crimson Roman damask, as in the library, there were a few steel engravings and mezzotints and an early nineteenth century lithograph or two. Over his night-table, at the side of his bed, he had pinned a photograph of a detail of Benozzo Gozzoli's frescoes in the Palazzo Riccardi, the detail of the three youths, and there was also a large framed photograph of Cranach's naïve Venus in this room. The piano stood in the drawing-room, near one of the windows, looking over the river. It was always open and the rack was littered with modern music: John Ireland's London Pieces, Béla Bartok's Three Burlesques, Gerald Tyrwhitt's Three Little Funeral Marches, music by Erik Satie, Darius Milhaud, Georges Auric, and Zoltan Kodaly. I remember one day he asked me to look at Theodor Streiche's Sprüche and Gedichte, with words by Richard Dehmel, the second of which he averred was the shortest song ever composed, consisting of but four bars.

It was a lovely house to lie about in, to talk in, to dream in. It was restful and quaint, offering a pleasing contrast to the eccentric modernity of the other homes I visited at this period. There was no electricity. The chandeliers burned gas but the favourite illumination was afforded by lamps with round glass globes of various colours, through which the soft light filtered.

On an afternoon in December, 1919, we were lounging in the drawing-room. Peter had curled himself into a sort of knot on a broad sofa with three carved walnut curves at the back. He had spread a knitted coverlet over his feet, for it was a little chilly, in spite of the fact that a wood fire was smouldering in the grate. On the table before him there was a highball glass, half-full of the proper ingredients, and sprawling beside him on the sofa, a magnificent blue Persian cat, which he called Chalcedony. George Moore and George Sand had long since perished of old age and Lou Matagot had been a victim of the laboratory explosion. There was a certain melancholy implicit in their absence. Nothing reminds us so irresistibly of the passing of time as the short age allotted on this earth to our dear cats. The pinchbottle and several bottles of soda, a bowl of cracked ice and a bowl of Fatima cigarettes, which both of us had grown to prefer, reposed conveniently on the table between us. I remember the increasing silence as the twilight fell and, how, at last, Peter began to talk.

I wanted to do so much, he began, and for a long time, during these past four years, it seemed to me that I had done so little. I remembered Zola's phrase: Mon œuvre, alors, c'était l'Arche, l'Arche immense! Hélas! ce que l'on rêve, et puis, après, ce que l'on exécute! At the beginning of the war, I was so very miserable, so unhappy, so *alone*. It seemed to me that I had been a complete failure, that I had accomplished nothing. . .

I must have raised a protesting hand, for he interjected, No, don't interrupt me. I am not complaining or asking for sympathy. I am explaining how I felt, not how I feel. I never spoke of it, of course, while I felt that way. I am only talking about it now because I have gone beyond, because, in a sense, at least, I understand. I am happier now, happier, perhaps, than I have ever been before, for in the past four years I have left behind my restlessness and achieved something like peace. I no longer feel that I have failed. Of course, I have failed, but that was because I was attempting to do something that I had no right to attempt. My cats should have taught me that. It is necessary to do only what one must, what one is forced by nature to do. Samuel Butler has said, and how truly, Nothing is worth doing or well done which is not done fairly easily, and some little deficiency of effort is more pardonable than any perceptible excess, for virtue has ever erred rather on the side of self-indulgence than of asceticism. . . And so, in the end, and after all I am still young, I have learned that I cannot write. Is a little experience too much to pay for learning to know oneself? I think not, and that is why, now, I feel more like a success than a failure, because, finally, I do know myself, and because I have left no bad work. I can say with Macaulay: There are no lees in my wine. It is all the cream of the bottle. . .

I have tried to do too much and that is why, perhaps, I have done nothing. I wanted to write a new Comédie Humaine. Instead, I have lived it. And now, I have come to the conclusion that that was all there was for me to do, just to live, as fully as possible. Sympathy and enthusiasm are something, after all. I must have communicated at least a shadow of these to the ideas and objects and people on whom I have bestowed them. Benozzo Gozzoli's frescoes—now, don't laugh at what I am going to say, because it is true when you understand it—are just so much more precious because I have loved them. They will give more people pleasure because I have given them my affection. This is something; indeed, next to the creation of the frescoes, perhaps it is everything.

There are two ways of becoming a writer: one, the cheaper, is to discover a formula: that is black magic; the other is to have the urge: that is white magic. I have never been able to discover a new formula; I have worked with the formulæ of other artists, only to see the cryptogram blot and blur under my hands. My manipulation of the mystic figures and the cabalistic secrets has never raised the right demons. . .

What is there anyway? All expression lifts us further away from simplicity and causes unhappiness. . . Material, scientific expression: flying-machines, moving pictures, and telegraphy are simply disturbing. They add nothing valuable to human life. Any novelist who invokes the aid of science dies a swift death. Zola's novels are stuffed with theories of heredity but ideas about heredity change every day. The current craze is for psychoanalytic novels, which are not half so psychoanalytic as the books of Jane Austen, as posterity will find out for itself. . . Art in this epoch is too self-conscious. Everybody is striving to do something *new*, instead of writing or painting or composing what is natural. . . Even the disturbing irony and pessimism of Anatole France and Thomas Hardy add nothing to life. We shall be happier if we go back to the beginning. . .

The great secret is the cat's secret, to do what one *has* to do. Let IT do it, let IT, whatever IT is, flow through you. The writer should say, with Sancho Panza, De mis viñas vengo, no sé nada. Labanne, in Le Chat Maigre, cries: Art declines in the degree that thought develops. In Greece, in the time of Aristotle, there were only sculptors. Artists are inferior beings. They resemble pregnant women; they give birth without knowing why. And again, to quote my beloved Samuel Butler, No one understands how anything is done unless he can do it himself; and even then he probably does not know how he has done it. I might add that very often he does not know what he has done. Sterne wrote Tristram Shandy to ridicule his personal enemies. Dickens began Pickwick to give the artist, Seymour, an opportunity to draw Cockney sportsmen and he concluded it in high moral fervour, with the ambition to wipe out bribery and corruption at elections, unscrupulous attorneys, and Fleet Prison. To Cervantes, Don Quixote was a burlesque of the high-flown romantic literature of his period. To the world, it is one of the great romances of all time. . .

You see, I am beginning to understand why I haven't written, why I cannot write. . . That is why I am unhappy no longer, why I am more peaceful, why I do not suffer. But, and now a strange, quavering note sounded in his voice, if I had found a new formula, who knows what I might have done?

He turned his face away from me towards the back of the sofa. The cat was purring heavily, almost like the croupy breathing of a child. It was quite dark outside, and there was no light in the room save for the flicker that came from the dying embers. There was a long silence. In trying afterwards to reckon its length, I judged it must have been fully half an hour before I spoke. It was a noise that broke the charm of the stillness. The dead end of the log split over the andirons and fell into the grate.

Peter, I began.

He did not move.

Peter. . . I rose and bent over him. The clock struck six. The cat stirred uneasily, rose, stretched his enormous length; then gave a faint but alarmingly portentous mew and leaped from the couch.

Peter!

He did not answer me.

April 29, 1921
New York.

THE END

A Note About the Author

Carl Van Vechten (1880–1964) was an American photographer, writer, and patron of the Harlem Renaissance. Born in Cedar Rapids, Iowa, Van Vechten was raised in a wealthy, highly educated family. After graduating from high school, he enrolled at the University of Chicago to study art and music, and spent much of his time writing for the college newspaper. In 1903, he took up a position as a columnist for the *Chicago American*, but was fired three years later for his difficult writing style. He moved to New York in 1906 to work as a music critic for *The New York Times*, focusing on opera and taking a leave of absence to travel through Europe the following year. Van Vechten's work as a critic coincided with the careers of some of the twentieth century's greatest artists—the dancer Isadora Duncan; Russian prima ballerina Anna Pavlovna; and Gertrude Stein, a writer and one of Van Vechten's closest friends. Van Vechten, who wrote an influential essay titled "How to Read Gertrude Stein," would become Stein's literary executor following her death in 1946. He is perhaps most notable for his promotion and patronage of some of the Harlem Renaissance's leading artists, including Paul Robeson and Richard Wright. In addition to his photographic portraits of such figures as Langston Hughes, Ella Fitzgerald, Zora Neale Hurston, Marcel Duchamp, and Frida Kahlo, Van Vechten was the author of several novels, including *Peter Whiffle: His Life and Works* (1922) and *Firecrackers: A Realistic Novel* (1925).

A Note from the Publisher

Spanning many genres, from non-fiction essays to literature classics to children's books and lyric poetry, Mint Edition books showcase the master works of our time in a modern new package. The text is freshly typeset, is clean and easy to read, and features a new note about the author in each volume. Many books also include exclusive new introductory material. Every book boasts a striking new cover, which makes it as appropriate for collecting as it is for gift giving. Mint Edition books are only printed when a reader orders them, so natural resources are not wasted. We're proud that our books are never manufactured in excess and exist only in the exact quantity they need to be read and enjoyed.

bookfinity™

Discover more of your favorite classics with Bookfinity™.

- Track your reading with custom book lists.
- Get great book recommendations for your personalized Reader Type.
- Add reviews for your favorite books.
- AND MUCH MORE!

Visit **bookfinity.com** and take the fun Reader Type quiz to get started.

Enjoy our classic and modern companion pairings!

Classic & Modern

Printed in the USA
CPSIA information can be obtained
at www.ICGtesting.com
JSHW082349140824
68134JS00020B/1965

9 781513 282268